BAD GIRLS

Also by Cynthia Voigt

BAD GIRLS

CYNTHIA VOIGT

SCHOLASTIC
HARDCOVER

Scholastic Inc. New York

Library of Congress Cataloging-in-Publication Data
Bad girls / Cynthia Voigt.
p.   cm.
Summary: After meeting on the first day in Mrs. Chemsky's fifth-grade
class, Margalo and Mikey help each other in and out of trouble, as they try to
maintain a friendship while each asserts her independence.
ISBN 0-590-60134-2
[1. Schools — Fiction.   2. Friendship — Fiction.
3. Behavior — Fiction.]   I. Title.
PZ7.V874Bad   1996
[Fic] — dc20   95-16168
                                                                      CIP
                                                                      AC
12 11 10 9 8 7 6 5 4 3 2   7 8 9/9 0 1/0

Printed in the U.S.A.   37

First printing, April 1996

*For Regina Griffin — even if she was a good girl
who didn't even want to be bad.
Because whatever their gender, age, status, situation, attitude,
or role in the story, she sees the characters alive.*

Contents

1

Margalo, Meet Mikey
Mikey, Meet Margalo

They said later that they were friends from the first minute of fifth grade, from the very first. "As soon as we met we were best friends," they both said, and they believed it, too.

What actually happened is: It started because of Mrs. Chemsky. Everybody said Mrs. Chemsky was the strictest teacher at Washington Street Elementary and this was a true thing to say. Some people even said she was the strictest teacher in any of the four elementary schools in Newtown, and some said she was the strictest in all of the schools in Newtown, including both junior highs, and the high school, too. *And* they had older brothers and sisters to prove it.

Certainly, Mrs. Chemsky kept strict order in her

fifth-grade classroom. The papers and pictures on Mrs. Chemsky's bulletin boards kept to straight horizontal lines and straight vertical lines. The desks in Mrs. Chemsky's classroom stood in straight lines across the floor. The books in their shelves were arranged alphabetically by author and the students were assigned alphabetically to their seats. In alphabetical order, Elsinger came just before Epps. Their two names, written in careful italic lettering on a folded piece of heavy white construction paper, waited on top of side-by-side desks, on the first day of school in Mrs. Chemsky's fifth-grade classroom, which is how it really started.

Margalo Epps would never have said so, but she was relieved to see that she had an assigned seat. She'd stood for a minute in the classroom doorway, just looking at the layout. She ignored the groups of old friends gathered together and noted instead the way the doorway into the hall — where she was standing — faced the back of a big, square classroom. Three windows, with bookshelves under them, ran along the opposite wall. Through the windows she could see a playground, and white clouds in a blue sky. There was a door leading outside at the end of that wall, and on the wall next to it a double row of coat hooks, and beside that the cubbies. Some of the coat hooks had a jacket or sweater on them. Some of the cubbies had a brown bag or books in them.

The desks were the kind where the seat is attached by an arm to the writing top, and the only storage space is a shelf under the seat. That was Margalo's least favorite kind of school desk. The teacher had a big wooden desk, a real desk, set right at the center of the front of the room. Chalkboards lined the wall behind her. Bulletin boards were on the wall facing the coat hooks and cubbies.

The teacher was seated at her desk. The teacher was a woman, who was not young, who neither colored nor curled her short hair, who ignored everything in the room except the papers she was reading.

Margalo sighed, dreading the day. *Sighed dreadfully*, she said to herself, trying to cheer herself up enough to take that first step into the room.

Then she noticed the folded paper on each desktop, like a doll's pup tent. Two words in dark capital letters were written on each paper. Names. There was assigned seating. Margalo sighed again, this time with relief.

She found her desk in the second row and hastily sat down, put the new *Star Trek* lunch box on the shelf under the seat, opened her new blue (should she have gotten red?) loose-leaf notebook, and pretended she was busy. Margalo pretended that nothing in the classroom could distract her from the important writing she was doing in the seat that had been assigned to her by her name, Margalo Epps, in alphabetical order.

Mikey didn't care where she sat. Also, she already had doubts about this teacher, who had hair the color of potato skins — a nonevent hair color. Hair color wasn't anything to do with age. One of Mikey's grandmothers had red hair, dyed. The other one had white hair, dyed. Her hair wasn't to do with however old this teacher was; it was to do with being the kind of person who saw herself as having short, potato-colored hair.

Between that and the way the desks were arranged in straight lines, with names on cards on the desks, names in alphabetical order — Mikey wasn't at all sure about this whole school year. She grabbed her name card and stuffed it into her pocket, then sat down. She set her *Sesame Street* lunch box — the same lunch box she'd had since the first day of school in first grade — on the tray under the desk seat, so Bert and Ernie were on top. Bert and Ernie always cheered her up, and if they didn't work, there was always Grover, on the other side. Grover could cheer her up higher than anything else, so she saved him for real need.

Mikey looked at the girls in the desks down from hers, the first in a puffy-sleeved checked dress, not the littlest bit nervous as she wrote in her big loose-leaf notebook, the next in a scoop-necked cotton T-shirt, wearing a heart-shaped locket. Mikey looked from one neighbor to the other and thought that she might need a lot of cheering up this year.

She hated the first day of school.

Mikey pulled her assignment notebook out of the back pocket of her jeans. Black, it was shiny black, and that made her feel almost OK. She shook free the little golf pencil she'd fitted into the coils. On the inside cover she wrote her name.

Actually, she wrote her initials. ME.

Mikey's initials said ME. Sometimes she wrote them all over the place, ME — ME — ME — ME — ME, right-side up, sideways, upside down, in arches, all over the page. Doing that sometimes cheered her up even more than Grover and Bert and Ernie all added together.

On this occasion, however, in this notebook, Mikey figured she had better lie low a little, and she wrote it just once, in the dead center of the inside top cover. ME.

The desk on her right stayed empty; some boy named Justin. On her left, the blonde girl a desk away fingered her locket and talked to her friends, and talked. The girl next to Mikey was still writing away, dressed up new for the first day of school, just like all the other dumb girls in the class. Brown straight hair she kept shoving behind her ear, before she went back to filling in the blanks at the front of her notebook. Mikey stared, to see how the girl would take it, and wondered what she was writing with such concentration.

Me. That's what Margalo was writing. Those were her initials, and that was her. The other girl was staring at her, so Margalo stared back, and the girl flipped her little black notebook closed.

Margalo wished she'd gotten a little notebook, for assignments, and brought just the one little notebook for the first day of school. She wished she'd made her mother let her wear jeans, too, not this dumb dress. She looked down, hating the big checks on the big, hated skirt, and saw two friendly faces looking up at her. She said, "That's Bert and Ernie."

"What did you expect?" the girl asked.

Margalo didn't know what she had done to make this girl so angry at her, but she didn't wait around to find out. She went back to filling in her street address, as if she had never said anything; but she couldn't remember the phone number.

How could she have forgotten her phone number? She'd memorized it, over and over.

No, now she could remember it, and she filled it in, shaping each numeral carefully, going as slowly as she could, wishing the teacher would say it was time for the school day to begin.

"I've had this lunch box since first grade," the girl said. The girl was heavyset, and her braid was so long it hung down until almost her waist.

Margalo tucked her hair back behind her ear. She was trying to grow it, and it was a lot of trouble. "I get a new one every year," she said. "The old ones get lost," she explained. "Because the little kids use them for campouts. In the summer. Or picnics," she said. "Sometimes they use them for both, until they get lost," she said. "The lunch boxes, not the little kids, get lost," she explained. She knew what an airhead she sounded like. She didn't need this girl smirking at her to know that. Obviously, the girl never thought to think that Margalo might sound that way on purpose. "Is something bothering you?" Margalo asked.

"You have a problem with my face?" Mikey answered. What was this girl's problem?

They stopped looking at each other, stopped talking, pretended to be checking their notebooks.

Other students kept entering the room, and ignoring the teacher where she sat behind her desk. Some of the other fifth-graders stood around, looking at everybody else who was already in the room, staring at anyone who was coming into the room. The groups of girls talked steadily, but the groups of boys would talk in bursts, until somebody said something funny enough so all of them could laugh at it.

Then they didn't say anything for a while. The girls talked like running water, somebody always having something to say and the rest listening, answering. The boys talked like a football game, waiting and watching, then bursting into action until they stopped, dead.

The minute hand on the clock over the door moved on towards 8:30.

"Listen," Mikey finally said, and turned in her chair to face Margalo. "I didn't mean —"

At the same time, practically exactly, Margalo was turning around to say, "I'm sorry, I —"

"That's OK," they both said, both of them feeling pretty dumb. But they were the only people either one of them came close to knowing in the room, so neither one wanted to quarrel.

"I'm Mikey Elsinger," Mikey said. "We have the same initials." She pointed to the folded paper with the girl's name on it, Margalo Epps. "See?" She pointed to the inside of her notebook, ME.

Margalo's eyes got rounder, and surprised. She turned her big notebook around, so Mikey could see what she had written there, on the line marked *Name*.

Me, she had written.

She had written it like an ordinary word, though. Not like a shout.

"We do the same thing," Margalo said. "With our initials."

Mikey thought it might look more cool the way Margalo did it.

"And we both have brown hair, and brown eyes. We both don't wear glasses. I'm five-two, how tall are you?" Margalo asked.

"Four foot eight."

Margalo kept talking away, filling the air with words. "I like that little notebook," she said. "My mother says mine was more value for the money, which is something she always likes to talk about. More bang for the bucks." Margalo grimaced, to apologize for her mother. "But I'd rather have a small one. Not just for assignments, either. Do you have brothers or sisters? I have six. But a lot of them are halves or steps."

"I'm an only child," Mikey said.

"When's your birthday? Mine was March, and it was snowing so hard my mother almost didn't make it to the hospital. I was almost born in a car because the roads were so bad. This was in New York. That's where they were, my mother and dad, in Rochester, New York, when I was born."

"You're not going to believe this," Mikey warned her.

"I believe everything," Margalo answered, and

this time she smiled right back when Mikey laughed at her. "Believe what?" she asked.

"So was I," Mikey announced.

Margalo's face went blank, the way a face does when it has just caught on. "Oh."

"No, I don't mean that. I mean, so was I born in Rochester."

"Oh," Margalo said again, but differently. "In Rochester? In March? You were? Then we're practically twins," Margalo said.

"Not March, July. My dad used to work for Eastman."

"Mine was a musician. We were passing through. My parents were, that is. I wasn't. I was just . . . being born. Almost in a car. Probably a station wagon. My mother always has a station wagon."

"Mine likes sedans," Mikey said.

"Weird, isn't it? Us being born in the same place. In the same year. Having the same initials that we write the same way."

Mikey realized something. "I have a middle name, too."

"I don't," said Margalo. "If I get married, I'd just lose it anyway. My mother says. Because, she did, and then when she got married again it was even farther away, and Gregory is her third so she couldn't ever see any sense in giving me a middle name."

"I hate mine," Mikey said. "I hate most of my

names. All of them, in fact." She smiled one of her mean smiles, to show how much she hated her names: "I'd like to kill them, all three. I'm going to change them all when I'm old enough."

"How old is that?" Margalo asked. When Mikey smiled that way, she looked mean, and dangerous — maybe evil. Margalo wanted to be her friend.

"Eighteen. Only eight years."

Margalo didn't say what she was thinking, which was, "Eight whole years." And when she saw how long Mikey's braid was, she almost wanted to give up on ever growing her hair long enough. She'd never get hair that long. When she looked at Mikey's cotton sweater, not bought new for the first day of school, she was glad she'd let her mother buy her a new dress, with a skirt that flared out after a belted waist. Margalo pulled the skirt down over her knees.

"My mother tried to get me to wear a dress," Mikey said. "To make a good impression." She gave Margalo another look at her smile. See if Margalo scared off easy.

"So what?" Margalo said, then added quickly, "We just moved here, did you? Because you're new, too, aren't you?" Before Mikey could answer whatever she would have answered, the teacher pushed her chair back, and stood up. The teacher didn't say anything. She just stood there behind her desk, while the rest of the class quickly seated themselves.

Margalo looked at Mikey. They realized it at the same time: This was a strict teacher.

It was the kind of thing kids always knew. New students in a class picked it up right away from the way old students acted. Old students came to school the first day already knowing it.

The whole classroom got quiet.

"My name is," the teacher announced, and then turned to write on the board behind her with a long piece of chalk, "Mrs. Chemsky."

She stepped aside to show her name, written on the green chalkboard in rounded script.

"We have thirty-one boys and girls in our class this year," she said. Mrs. Chemsky wore thick-soled shoes, and she made no shoe-noises when she walked back and forth at the front of the room. "The most desirable size for a fifth-grade class is no more than twenty-four boys and girls. Because there are so many of you, in order to get the necessary material covered this school year, your behavior will have to be exemplary," she said.

"I trust that you know that word? If not, I will let you know the meaning of exemplary behavior."

Mikey's smile caught the teacher's eye. Her *Oh-yeah?* smile caught the teacher's now-suspicious eye. *Uh-oh*, Mikey thought, but she kept her smile on her face. And she thought *Uh-oh* with a kind of

excited feeling, like when she was goalie and somebody kicked a really hard shot at her.

Mrs. Chemsky told them how to answer to their
names during morning roll call, and then she
opened the big gray attendance book to start the
first day of school. "On this first morning, I will skip
over the new boys and girls," she announced. Mrs.
Chemsky was the kind of teacher who liked making
announcements. "We want a chance to hear from
them later. Individually."

Margalo and Mikey looked at each other: bad
news.

"Karen Blackaway," Mrs. Chemsky said.

"Here," answered a blonde girl in the front row.

On a page in her notebook, Margalo wrote down
the names. She had good handwriting, Mikey noticed, well-shaped letters, well-spaced words.

"Joanna Burns."

"Here," answered a dark-haired girl, who looked
and sounded so nervous it was hard to believe she
was an old student.

"Louis Caselli."

"Absent."

The class didn't dare to laugh. Mrs. Chemsky
waited, fifteen full fat staring seconds. Louis Caselli
was a square, soft-cheeked boy, with a self-satisfied
grin on his round face.

"Louis Caselli," Mrs. Chemsky said again.

He gave in. "Here," he said. "Mrs. Chemsky? I have a question."

"In this classroom, Louis, when you have a question you raise your hand. Then, when you have been called on, you may speak. Yes, Louis?"

"What about, if someone has to go to the bathroom?"

The titters were quickly muffled.

"Then you raise your hand and ask to be excused," Mrs. Chemsky said. "Yes, Louis?"

"May I be excused?"

"No." Mrs. Chemsky raised her voice to call the next name. "Salvatore Caselli."

"Here."

"Yes, Salvatore?" she called on him.

"May I please be excused?"

"No," she said. "Yes, Louis?"

"I really have to go," Louis said.

"I am sorry to hear that," Mrs. Chemsky said. "Veronica Caselli?"

On the side of her notebook page where Mikey could see it, Margalo wrote *Do you think they're triplets?*

Mikey reached over to write *How nows?* under the question. *Trublemakers,* she added.

It took Margalo a brief minute to work it out.

Then she wrote *Agreed,* and didn't add anything about Mikey's bad spelling.

Mikey reached over to write *stepbr* —. Something made her look up, caught. *Uh-oh,* Mikey thought again. She drew her hand back to her own desk and smiled again. This was her harmless smile, the *I'm-just-a-harmless-girl* smile. Mikey had a whole closetful of smiles, one for every occasion.

The last boy in alphabetical order was David Thomas, and the last girl was Lindsey Westerburg. Wherever Margalo went to school, the place was littered with Lindseys, and boys whose names began with the letter J. This class also had two people named Smith, three named Caselli, and even one person whose first and last initials were the same, Rhonda Ransom.

"Now," Mrs. Chemsky said, "for our eight new students."

Margalo wrote at the top of the paper 32, and circled it. Mikey reached over to write 31. Margalo counted the names again, and erased Mikey's number. She erased the 2 in her number. She filled in a 1 and retraced the circle.

"I am going to ask each new student to answer 'Here,' and then to stand, so we can all see you, and get to know something about you."

Embarrassment rose into the room, like a bad

smell. None of the new students looked at anybody else. Margalo looked up at Mrs. Chemsky, who happened to be looking at her right then, as if Mrs. Chemsky wondered if Margalo was the source of the smell.

"Each one of you can tell us something about yourself," Mrs. Chemsky said. "Something to help us get to know you. Something brief, please. The first day of school is, as you know, a shortened day so we have no time to waste," she said. "I call on Keith Adams," she said.

"Here," said the boy in the right-hand desk of the first row, closest to the hall door.

"Stand up, Keith," Mrs. Chemsky reminded him.

He looked perfectly normal, in soccer shorts and a Packers T-shirt, and Reeboks. He had sandy-colored hair and a good tan. He looked unhappy.

You're next, Margalo wrote on her notebook page.

I now. Mikey smiled, the *You're-not-scaring-me* smile. *Then you*.

Thanx, in sarcastic writing.

Keith Adams was saying something about having been in the C.D. Brooks School last year, playing in soccer games against Washington. Some of the boys in the class made threatening noises, and Louis Caselli asked if Keith was the one who kicked his little brother in the kidney, and Keith denied it, denied that anything like that ever even happened, before Mrs. Chemsky told Louis not to interrupt, please.

Keith sat down, and his cheeks were pink.

"Michelle Elsinger," Mrs. Chemsky called.

"Here," Mikey answered, and stood up boldly, her hands jammed into the rear pockets of her jeans. "My name's Mikey," she said to the class. "Nobody calls me Michelle. Not if they know what's good for them." She sat down, satisfied.

"Stand up again, please, Michelle," Mrs. Chemsky said.

Mikey stood.

And glared at the teacher.

"There are no nicknames used in this classroom," Mrs. Chemsky announced. "Also, we don't threaten violence to one another. So is there anything else about yourself you would like to tell us?"

"I don't think so," Mikey said. What Mrs. Chemsky didn't know was that when Mikey got mad, her brain got cool. "However, can I ask you — please," she added, just the way the teacher did, "to call me Miss Elsinger, when you talk to me, in this classroom?" she said, pronouncing those three words just the way the teacher had. "We call *you* Mrs. Chemsky."

Margalo watched the teacher. She was pretty sure she could guess what was going on in the teacher's head. Mrs. Chemsky wanted to say that wasn't possible, and she wanted to say it was a ridiculous request, and not exemplary at all, but she couldn't say what she wanted. "I can try," was what she finally said.

Mikey had her hands jammed into her back pockets, in nervous fists, but she smiled her cool-cat smile for the teacher. *Nothing-fazes-me,* that smile said.

"You may sit down now," Mrs. Chemsky said, adding on at the end, with emphasis, "Miss," she waited a beat, "Elsinger."

There were little giggles around the classroom at the way that sounded. Mrs. Chemsky looked pleased with her own joke.

"Margalo Epps," Mrs. Chemsky called, too quickly for Mikey to say anything more.

Margalo stood, and smoothed the skirt of her dress, and opened her mouth to say something about herself. Margalo didn't look nervous at all, Mikey thought, resentfully. She looked tall, and tidy.

"What do you answer?" Mrs. Chemsky reminded Margalo.

"Oh. Sorry."

Margalo sat down.

"Here," Margalo said.

Then she stood up again, and tucked hair behind her right ear, and tucked hair behind her left ear.

She smoothed her skirt and looked at Mrs. Chemsky, apparently waiting for permission to speak.

"Do you want to tell us something about yourself?" Mrs. Chemsky asked, the way she might talk to someone very young or very dim-witted.

"No. But I have to, don't I?" Margalo asked. She heard people stirring to attention, which was more like it. "My name is Margalo, after the bird. Not a real bird. There's no real bird named the Margalo. The bird in *Stuart Little*, remember her? She goes off and he goes after her? In his little car? But he doesn't find her," Margalo said, and started to sit down, pretending she hadn't heard the muffled laughter. Then she got up again. "I'm sorry. I wasn't finished. My mother named me Margalo after my father." She gave that a minute. "Because he used to run off. He was a musician, but he's not my father anymore."

By this time, the whole class was smothering laughter. Margalo looked right at Mrs. Chemsky with big brown innocent eyes.

Mrs. Chemsky looked back with narrowed doubting eyes.

Margalo started to sit down again, but stopped halfway and straightened up again. Everybody waited. Mrs. Chemsky — her mouth half open to call on the next person — waited, too.

Margalo changed her mind and sat down without saying anything.

Mrs. Chemsky never laughed in class. She would let a class laugh by itself for about five seconds and then she would start staring at people. Her eyes would sort of bulge out of their sockets and her lips would get straighter and narrower. It didn't take long for a class to settle down when Mrs. Chemsky wanted it to. If Mrs. Chemsky didn't think something was funny she wouldn't even smile; and she almost never thought anything was funny.

"Lindsey Joynes," Mrs. Chemsky said.

"Here," an African-American girl said. She stood up to tell them that she and her mother had moved to Newtown to live with her aunt, and then she sat down, and twined her fingers together, and looked as if she wished she hadn't said that.

3 Lindseys! Margalo wrote. *!!!* she wrote.

Mikey stuck to the point. *That's funy*, she wrote.

"Hadrian Klenk," Mrs. Chemsky announced, and glared at her class, to keep them from saying anything.

"Here."

A short skinny boy with a dark buzz stood up. His pants were belted tight at the waist and his T-shirt was striped in green and brown and white. "I'm named after an emperor of the late Roman Empire," he said. "It's weird," he apologized.

"I don't think it's weird," Mrs. Chemsky objected.

Hadrian Klenk was already sitting down. His hands covered his face.

You can't spell, Margalo wrote while Mikey watched.

"Miss Elsinger?" Mrs. Chemsky inquired. "Margalo? Do you think the rest of us could have your attention?"

Both of them looked up, neither said a word, and both smiled with more teeth than friendliness at the teacher. They could almost see what Mrs. Chemsky was thinking, "Uh-oh." They could almost see the letters going across her forehead, like an electronic billboard at a baseball stadium. U-H O-H.

"Joshua Rey," Mrs. Chemsky said.

"Yo."

"I beg your pardon?" Mrs. Chemsky asked.

They got through Henry Weisler and Derrie Zurlo without incident, except that Derrie Zurlo was chewing gum, which was not permitted in this classroom.

Then Mrs. Chemsky assigned them each a cubby, in alphabetical order, starting at the top left, and she gave them their textbooks. She told them to put their initials beside their names, in alphabetical order on the long printout, to show that they had received three books, math and science and social studies. "You are responsible for keeping these textbooks in good condition, all year," she warned her students. "I will help you meet that responsibility," she promised them. There were also three soft-bound workbooks — for math, for spelling, and for social studies. There was a grammar workbook, with lines for answering the grammar questions on each page, and there was a creative writing workbook, with lines for answering the creative writing questions on each page. Workbooks were given to students, but if they lost one they would have to pay to replace it, immediately, so the work could go on. "The readers, and the class sets of novels, I keep in the shelves behind my desk," Mrs. Chemsky announced to everyone. "These are recorded separately, because they are books that belong to this classroom rather than the school. Now, everyone — slowly, no need to rush and crowd — go find your cubby and put your new books into it. Then return to your seat. Let's see how quickly and efficiently we can do this task."

There was just enough time before snack recess, Mrs. Chemsky announced, to go over the rules. After the recess, Mrs. Chemsky reminded them, they would fill out the sign-up sheets for clubs and athletics, and then she would ask them to fill in a personal fact sheet, telling her about themselves, and their families, with a paragraph on the back about their favorite activity — not, of course, in-

cluding TV-watching ha-ha, she said — or their favorite vacation — "Just to get the juices flowing,"
she said. After that, and to end the day, she would
ask them to do a math worksheet. "So I can see
where we all are," she said, "especially the new students. Does everyone understand the schedule for
the rest of the day?"

Everybody did, so nobody said anything.

"I would like to hear a *Yes, Mrs. Chemsky,*" Mrs.
Chemsky said.

She heard it.

She also heard places where she didn't hear it,
and she stared first and longest at the Caselli boys.
Then she glanced in brief warning at the two girls.
Margalo and Mikey could almost hear what she was
thinking: "How bad can two fifth-grade girls be?"

"Everyone, open your notebooks," Mrs. Chemsky
said, "or take a sheet of paper. I want you to keep
what you are about to copy down, so plan to put it
in a safe place. I have paper and pencils for those of
you who could not remember what supplies are
necessary for school. Those who need to may come
up and get paper and pencil from my desk. Raise
your hands, I'll call on you and then you may come
up, one at a time. Yes, Louis, you first."

Everybody watched while the students who came
to school without proper supplies marched up to
the desk, in alphabetical order, and then marched

back, a sheet of paper in one hand, a sharpened pencil in the other. Margalo, without being asked, had quietly opened the rings of her notebook, lifted out three sheets of lined paper, passed them to Mikey and then, just as quietly, closed the rings. Mikey wrote on the top of Margalo's paper, *Thanks.* She'd have hated to have to walk up, and walk back. She'd have done it, but it would have been a pain.

Margalo erased the word. *Me,* she wrote, in the upper left-hand corner. *Rules,* she headed the page, in the center of the top line, and then she erased that, too. *Mrs. Chemsky's Rules,* she wrote.

Mikey wrote *ME* at the top right of her paper, and watched what Margalo was doing.

Margalo was erasing the heading of her paper for the second time.

Mrs. Chemsky was watching Margalo, and watching Mikey read what Margalo was writing. Ira Pliotes had just been called up to get a sheet of paper, and a pencil.

MRS. CHEMSKY'S MANY RULES, Margalo headed her paper.

"Derrie Zurlo, you may come up now," Mrs. Chemsky said. Derrie had sworn that it wasn't a nickname — "Call my mother, if you don't believe me. You can call her at work." Derrie had a pencil, she said, but she'd left her paper in her mother's car, along with her snack.

"I'm sure someone will share her snack with you," Mrs. Chemsky promised.

RULES, Mikey wrote on the top line, centered. Underneath it she added *Or HOW 2 SERVIE FITH GRAPE.*

Margalo reached over, with her pencil.

"Margalo?"

"Yes, Mrs. Chemsky."

"What are you doing?"

Margalo hesitated, and thought. "Helping," she said.

Mrs. Chemsky tried to think of what to say. She thought of, "You're not helping *me*."

Margalo had finished erasing the *p* in *grape* and filling in *d*.

"Oh, sorry," Margalo said. "I'll try not to do it again," she said.

Mikey crossed out the top of the *d*. She added down a tail, to make it a *p* again, and wished her little golf pencil came with an eraser.

"I will write the rules on the board," Mrs. Chemsky told the class, and showed everyone the piece of chalk she would write with. "You will copy them down from the board, onto your paper. I will expect you to remember these rules, and abide by them."

She waited.

"Yes, Mrs. Chemsky," many voices said, but not

the two Mrs. Chemsky was listening for. "I'm in fifth *grape*," Mikey was muttering to Margalo.

Mrs. Chemsky had seventeen rules to copy down, which took her class anywhere from one page for the neatest and most careful copiers, to three pages for most of the boys, and Mikey. Mrs. Chemsky had Forbidding Rules, like No Talking, and No Gum Chewing, and No Bare Feet. She had Performance Rules, like Homework must be handed in on the morning of the day it is due, and Any missed test or quiz will be taken on the student's first day back in school. She had Behavior Rules, like If you are absent you must bring a note from home the first day back, and You may not be excused on Friday until both your cubby and desk areas have been approved. Because the basement cafeteria was closed until the school had removed asbestos in the ceiling insulation, "about which your parents have received letters," Mrs. Chemsky said, there were three Lunch Rules added on: About neatness (pro), and trading (con), and what could be done if a student forgot his lunch.

"Or hers," Rhonda Ransom remarked to the teacher.

"If you have something to say, raise your hand and wait to be called on, Rhonda," Mrs. Chemsky said, patiently, and then added, "That is, if you have anything it is important for us to hear."

Margalo copied down the rules in neat round handwriting that stayed steady on the line. It took her only one and a half pages. Mikey wrote them down in neat spiky handwriting that stayed steady on the line, too; but somehow it always took her more lines. At the top right-hand corner of each of her three pages — where, under the requirements set out in rule eight, her name and the date were supposed to be put — underneath her initials she wrote *Miss Elsinger,* and underneath that, lined up straight, *Grape 5.*

This time, she let Margalo see her *Just-plain-funny* smile, the one before she just plain burst out laughing, unless, of course, circumstances forbade out-loud laughter — circumstances or Mrs. Chemsky.

"Miss Elsinger? May I ask what you are doing?" Mrs. Chemsky asked.

Heads turned to see.

"What you said," Mikey said. "I'm putting my name on the top of the paper. And my grape," she added.

Beside her, Margalo was practically bright red.

"I'm sorry, your what?" Mrs. Chemsky asked, in a warning voice.

"My grape."

"You mean, your grade," Mrs. Chemsky corrected Mikey. The class was all laughing now, or trying not to. "But it's not your grade you put at the top of the paper, under your name. It's the date. Rule eight," she reminded them all, and pointed her chalk at where rule eight was written out on the board. "Now. Before we all go outside for recess, you may go to your cubbies and take down your lunch boxes, to have your snack. Yes, Louis?"

"May I please be excused?" Louis Caselli asked, and Mrs. Chemsky was glad to hear the predictable request. "Yes you may, Louis. And so may anyone else who needs to. There is no need to ask permission to leave the classroom during recess. Now. Does anyone have a snack to share with Derrie?"

Both Mikey and Margalo ate their snacks slowly. The black cloud of recess hung over the new students, ready to drop down lightning, and cold rain, and bad feelings. Everybody knew that. It wasn't just the prospect of standing alone where everybody could see that you had no friends. The really scary possibility was that — for some reason, some reason you had no idea about — everyone might positively dislike you, and want to stand near you and say mean things, and want to embarrass you.

Probably, that wouldn't happen. Everyone knew that. People weren't that bad, everybody knew.

But.

But when you were new, you just didn't know.

So.

Margalo and Mikey lingered over their snacks. Mikey had an orange, and some oversized brownies that looked homemade. Margalo had a packet of Wingdings and a banana. They were the last to leave the classroom. Mrs. Chemsky had left them alone by then, with instructions to clean up after their snacks and then go outside. "I'll be back," she warned them.

They watched her leave the room, and listened to her walk down the hallway, until she couldn't hear whatever they said. Margalo said, "Maybe she smokes."

"Schools are no smoking zones."

"Maybe she had to be excused," Margalo said. She got up out of her seat to throw away the banana peel and the Wingding wrappings.

Mikey smiled her put-down smile, *Do-you-really-think-that's-funny?* She closed her lunch box. She wondered if she should have worn a dress for the first day of school, or at least a good shirt. She gathered her orange peels into a pile and slipped out of her seat to throw them into the trash.

Margalo was smoothing down the checked skirt of her dress. "Well," she said.

Mikey pulled down on her cotton sweater. "I guess," she said.

They would feel safer together, although neither admitted that.

Margalo tucked hair behind both ears, a two-handed tuck. "I guess I should have worn jeans. But my mother wanted me to wear a new dress. She always does, because she never had one for the first day of school, so she always takes us all shopping the week before school starts, all of us together. It's a family thing."

"I almost wore a dress," Mikey said. It wasn't true but it sounded good, so she added, "Or a skirt."

They were out the rear door by then, outside. The sun shone and the air was heavy with humidity. Kids ran around all over the place, jabbering and laughing and calling out. The two new girls walked slowly around the side of the building. At the front there was a grassy lawn, with three tall swing sets and a round jungle gym set into the ground. Mostly little children played at the front, and many of them clung to their teachers. Brick pathways led around both sides of the building to the playground area at the back. There, basketball hoops stood at either end of the paved area and a flat dirt field with two soccer goals set up on it was beside that. A couple of teachers stood talking, monitoring the back playground.

It looked like the older grades went out back. Mikey recognized the male Casellis, with their stocky bodies and thick dark hair, leading a pack of boys down the dirt field. Louis and Salvatore stayed ahead of the rest, passing a soccer ball back and forth between them. An opposing boy pack ran up to try to take the ball away from the Casellis.

Girls stood at the side of the soccer field, pretending to talk, pretending not to be watching the boys play.

"It's sort of a slow game," Mikey said.

"Soccer?" Margalo asked. She'd always heard that soccer was a fast game. Shuffleboard was slow. Baseball was slow, or at least, the game progressed slowly. But soccer had everybody running around, fast.

"No, not soccer, or it shouldn't be. But this one is."

The ball careened off Louis's foot and towards some watching girls. The girls backed politely away, except Mikey. Mikey ran forward. She bent over, picked up the ball, and then drop-kicked it, over the heads of the Casellis, over the heads of their whole team.

All the boys on the field followed the ball back down the field, running, complaining that it wasn't fair, complaining that she wasn't playing, complaining that only the goalie could put hands on the ball.

"You want to join in?" Mikey asked Margalo, and ran out onto the field.

Margalo wasn't about to do that, not with a new dress. She wouldn't have even in jeans, or shorts, because she was pretty sure this was a boys' pickup game. She was pretty sure that girls weren't supposed to play.

Also, she wasn't good at sports. Margalo didn't want to look like a jerk trying to play sports on the first day of school when she wasn't any good.

Mikey placed herself in the middle of the field, and the Casellis — having regained possession of the ball — came towards her. The rest of Mikey's team backed away. They were hoping for an error. They were waiting for an error to be made. They were hoping that Louis and Sal would miss a pass, and they were waiting to help out when that happened.

Mikey didn't wait. She charged. She made a sliding tackle against Louis Caselli. The ball went flying off to the side.

"Come on!" Mikey yelled to her team, scrambling to her feet. But by the time they figured out what she meant, and responded to her, it was too late. The Casellis were bringing the ball down the field again.

This time Louis and Sal tried to work it behind Mikey with a get and go, but she ran sideways, slanted backwards, and cut off the pass. She didn't have time to trap and kick it, however, so the best she could do was belt it out of bounds.

Everybody was panting, and many of the players were angry.

"Who said she could play?"

"Who says she can't?"

"It's against the rules."

"Why, because I'm a girl?"

"No, stupid. Because we already chose teams."

"And you weren't chosen for any team, Michelle," Louis Caselli said.

He and Mikey had faced off. His face was blotchy red, perhaps from all the running around. Sweat plastered his hair down his forehead, and he wiped it back.

Mikey was panting, too. "Not everybody will agree with you. If you ask anybody else's opinion," she told him. She smiled right into his face, a broad *What's-your-problem?* smile.

"Yeah, just because she tackled you."

"Just because she's better than you are."

"She's not," Sal protested. "You haven't even seen our best plays yet. You haven't even *seen* what we can do. For Pete's sake."

"So get off the field, Michelle," Louis said.

"Don't call me that."

"I'll call you whatever I want."

"Oh yeah?"

"Yeah."

"And if I don't like it?"

"You can lump it. Or you can tattletale to Mrs. Chemsky. Does Michelle . . . tell?" Louis asked. "Ha-ha. I'm a poet and I don't know it," he said, sneering right into Mikey's face.

Until she punched him.

Punch, in the nose. Wham.

It happened so quickly that Louis had no time to raise an arm for protection. It happened so quickly that nobody saw it starting.

"What —?"

"Did she —?"

"— what I think I saw?"

For a minute, everyone stood still. Absolutely.

Louis had his hands over his nose, and his eyes watered. Furiously.

"No fair," Sal said. "We can't hit *you*, and you know it."

Mikey turned to answer Sal and when her back was to him Louis grabbed her braid. He yanked back on it, with his whole arm, hard. Mikey wheeled around, pulling her hair out of Louis's hand, and Sal grabbed her braid, and jerked it. Mikey pulled it free, and turned again, trying to position herself where she could see them both. She smiled, the evil smile.

She held her braid against her chest. Her leg whipped out to give Sal a crack on the shins. She faced Louis, ready to punch him again.

Sal grabbed her braid.

That was too much for Margalo, who pushed her way into the little knotted group, and pushed Sal away, paying no attention to what people were saying.

"What's wrong with them?"

"On the first day —?"

"Don't they know —?"

"Maybe where they went to school before —?"

"Were they friends from before?"

Margalo's fighting style involved fists, but no punching. Margalo was a flailer. She flailed at anyone who was near enough to hit, and it wasn't long before the Casellis were hitting back and the girls on the sidelines protested. "You can't hit girls!" they said. They shoved against the backs and shoulders of the boys.

The boys, of course, wouldn't stand for that. So they shoved back, and moved around, everybody shoving everybody else. The boys shoved with shoulders first, then with the palms of their hands, until they found they were punching at the girls.

And the girls were punching back.

"Did you see what he did?"

"You can't do that!"

"Who says!"

"Did you see what she just did?"

"That's not fair!" Shove.

"Not fair!" Punch.

"Not" — kick — "fair!"

By the time the teachers on duty got them all separated, there were two bloody noses (one belonging to Margalo, but, luckily, there was red in the checks of her dress), half-a-dozen bruised shins and shoulders, and uncounted minor scrapes, cuts, abrasions, but no broken bones (although Louis Caselli squeezed his nose protectively), and no tears.

Margalo's dress had been ripped at the sleeve. The right sleeve hung down her arm. Tanisha Harris had a lip that was already ballooning up, and Veronica Caselli — "Only call me Ronnie, would *you* like do be called Veronica? All the Archie and Jughead jokes?" — was nursing a set of bruised knuckles. "I wasn't going to be on *their* side. I don't care if we are all cousins."

Of the thirty-one students in Mrs. Chemsky's class, eleven had been involved in the melee, as had eight students from the other fifth grade. There were some sixth-graders also in need of bandages, and even two fourth-grade boys. Most of the upper grades in Washington Street Elementary spent the rest of the short first day of school trying to figure out what they were going to say to their mothers when they got home.

Mrs. Chemsky had come out to help restore order, as had Ms Spalding, the other fifth-grade teacher. Also present was Mr. Delaney who was not only one of the adults on recess duty but was also the principal. He had never, he told them all in an impromptu speech, been so dismayed and disappointed on a first day of school. He had never seen students act like this before — ever — on a first day of school. Never once in his whole long career. He wanted to know just what had happened out here.

But nobody could remember.

"Who started this fight?"

Margalo stood beside Mikey, both of them with dusty scrapes on their knees, and dusty scrapes on their elbows. They glared at the two Casellis. Mikey's hands were still in fists, jammed in her pockets.

"Yes, Louis?" Mr. Delaney said.

"Actually, it was —" Louis Caselli started to say. Then he saw Mikey's face.

She was smiling at him.

"An accident," Louis Caselli said. He said, "I wasn't even there. I was in the boys' room."

* * *

Margalo and Mikey trailed behind at the end of the disgraced fifth- and sixth-graders. Mikey was glaring at Margalo.

Margalo held her ripped sleeve up over her shoulder and glared back. "Look what you did."

Mikey wiped a streak of dirt across her cheek. "I was fine until you butted in."

They didn't speak for the rest of the day.

It was lucky it was the first day of school, because the not-speaking only went on for another hour. During that time they were filling out math papers for Mrs. Chemsky, so it was probably good that they were angry. They would just have gotten into more trouble if they'd been getting along.

2

Are We Friends Yet?

"Pet Day," Mrs. Chemsky announced at the start of the second week of school, "for those of you who are new to Washington Street Elementary, is one of our high points of the year. Old students, don't you agree?"

"Yes, Mrs. Chemsky," they agreed. It was morning announcements.

"Remember Jimmy Fitzer's dog in second grade? Remember that Doberman?"

"That's enough, Louis," Mrs. Chemsky said.

"It was a weimaraner. And it went for your cocker spaniel, Ann, what's her name, Sweetie? Cutie-Pie? Honey-Bits?"

"Misty. Her name is Misty. You know my dog's name perfectly well, Justin Collingham. I don't know why you pretend you don't since when you come over to my house you say it's to see *her*."

"Guess we know who wears the pants in *that* couple," Louis said.

"I'm sure," Mrs. Chemsky said firmly, "that nobody is interested in old memories when we have announcements to read."

"What did the weimaraner do that was so bad?" Mikey asked this question of the class in general. She didn't want to speak to Louis Caselli personally unless her life depended on it; if terrorists were attacking the school, for example, and only Louis Caselli could save her life.

"Jimmy was such a wimp. He couldn't even hang on to his own dog's collar."

"The dog got away. He ran *loose*. Barking and snarling. Remember?"

"Ann peed her pants."

"I did *not*, Louis. I *never*."

"OK, maybe you just looked like it."

Mrs. Chemsky banged once on her desk with a twelve-inch wooden ruler. It sounded like a whip, cracking, or a gun, shooting. All the voices stopped.

Mrs. Chemsky stared at them for a few seconds. She stared hardest at Mikey. "We didn't need that question, Miss Elsinger," she announced. "But I'll answer it — for the benefit of all of the new students, since you were not here for the excitement.

Three years ago, on Pet Day, there was a dogfight involving half a dozen animals, all of whom got loose from their owners. They were the largest dogs."

"Except for the dachshund. He was mean. But he got creamed, remember?" Louis Caselli asked.

"It was," Mrs. Chemsky overrode Louis, "Mr. Delaney's first year as principal. He required fourteen stitches in the hospital emergency room, on his arm and his leg. He was very brave."

"So were you, Mrs. Chemsky," Annaliese Gittler said. "I remember it, you made us all go inside, but you stayed outside and you got a bucket — you remember this, Ronnie, you were in my class. Don't you remember watching through the window? Mrs. Chemsky filled the bucket with water and poured it all over the fighting dogs. You did it at least twice, Mrs. Chemsky. Running. You were brave, too."

"Not quite as brave as Mr. Delaney, but yes," Mrs. Chemsky said, "I did try to help out. However, the significant point for us is, if your pet is a dog, he or she must be brought to school by a parent, and may not arrive until after the lunch period. Also, if the dog has not had obedience training, he or she must stand no taller than the owner's knees."

"On a leash, too."

"Raise your hand, Rhonda, and wait to be called on, please. Yes, Louis?"

"Goldy's never been in a fight in her life, not once. I brought her last year."

"It's the rule, Louis. All dogs must be leashed."

"I brought her last year and everything went fine."

"We can discuss this after class, Louis. Remember, everyone, if your dog is over knee-height, I must have a certificate of obedience training. Yes, Noah?"

"What if it's not a dog. What if it's a wolf?"

"Are you bringing a wolf to Pet Day this year, Noah?"

"No, Mrs. Chemsky. I just wondered."

"Is anyone bringing a wolf to Pet Day this year? Class?"

Nobody was.

"Or a horse? If it rains and the parade is inside, horses can be dangerous," Noah asked.

"Are you bringing a horse, Noah?" Mrs. Chemsky asked.

"No, Mrs. Chemsky. I don't have a horse."

"Is anyone planning on bringing a horse to Pet Day this year? Class?"

Nobody was.

Mrs. Chemsky smiled.

The class smiled back, happily. Minutes were ticking by on the clock. Every minute that ticked by wasted meant one minute less that had to be waited through to get to recess.

"No more questions, Noah," Mrs. Chemsky said. "Remember, class, as you make your plans, that any pet which is not in some kind of container may not be brought to school until after lunch, but you want your pet to be in time for the Parade of Pets. I don't think I have to remind you that only the youngest grades are permitted to bring stuffed animals, do I?" she asked. "Now. Everyone. Take out your math homework, please, so we can see how we did on the word problems."

"Terrible."

"I tried, but I —"

"Easy, they were simple."

"Ask my mother, she'll tell you."

"— only got half of the first one done."

"I bet I've got them all right."

"It's not fair to give us so much homework right away. My father said."

Margalo and Mikey had both finished the assignment during class on Friday. They unfolded the math papers onto their desks. Each problem on Margalo's sheet was illustrated with a small drawing: Two cars traveled side by side, fruit was piled up in mounds of seven. At the top of *her* ditto sheet, Mikey had drawn a spaceship that dropped alien bombs onto all of the questions. She had drawn a row of soldiers at the bottom, firing up. The soldiers' weapons shot up comic-book-style balloons, which held the answers.

"What about Pet Day?" Mikey asked Margalo, under cover of rustling papers and complaining voices.

"What about it?"

"You could be my pet. Will you?"

Margalo laughed.

"Or I could be yours," Mikey said. "That would be better, anyway, because I'm shorter than you."

"Will you two girls *please* settle down?" Mrs. Chemsky asked.

This was Monday and Pet Day was Friday. "They don't like to give much time for people to get excited," Lindsey Westerburg explained, during morning snack recess. She was the Lindsey without a nickname. She wasn't the kind of person other people wanted to give a nickname to, unlike Eljay, who had been given that name about the second day of school, or Lynnie Mitchell. "Because," Lindsey explained to Mikey and Margalo, "kids get too excited, especially the little kids. The teachers want to keep excitement to a minimum. What are you bringing?"

"I'm not sure," Margalo said.

Lindsey was the kind of person you wanted to say no to, and keep things secret from.

"I'm thinking of my boa constrictor," Mikey volunteered.

"Oeeow, do you have snakes?" Lindsey squealed. "Oeeow."

Mikey smiled, a low-wattage mean smile, *I'm-meaner-than-you.*

Attracted by the squeals, which promised something interesting, people gathered around Mikey's desk; they stayed to talk about Pet Day.

Most people, Karen told Mikey and Margalo, brought dogs or cats. "Louis," she told them, "has a golden retriever that's his best friend." She laughed. "He even eats her dog biscuits. He says he likes them. Can you believe it?"

"He's just a liar."

"He just likes to show off to prove how great he is."

"He thinks."

"No," Ronnie Caselli said, and she would know because Louis was her cousin. "I mean, yes he does lie, and show off, but not about this."

"I bet," Mikey said.

"You can bet all you want," Ronnie said. "It's still true."

She turned around and called. "Lou? Louie?"

Louis strutted over.

He did strut, and everybody could see that, because he liked being called over across the classroom to where the girls were all watching him.

"Yeah?" he asked.

"They don't believe you eat dog biscuits," Ronnie said.

Mikey smiled a level-two mean smile, *Now-what're-you-going-to-do?*

Louis smiled a strutting smile back. "You mean Mee-shell doesn't believe it."

Mikey started to stand up and quarrel face-to-face, but Margalo joined in. "I don't believe it, either."

Mikey said, "I just don't think it's such a big deal. I've done it myself but I never bothered to boast about it."

"Yeah?" Louis asked. "Yeah? Well," he said, "if you notice, it wasn't me that brought it up, it was Ronnie here."

"Well," Margalo said, before anyone else had time to think of anything to answer, "how did Ronnie find out? Who told *her?*"

"Yeah," Ronnie said.

"Yeah," Mikey said, smiling her *You-lose* smile.

Louis challenged Mikey. "How do we know you're not lying?"

"I don't lie," she said.

"Like I believe *that*."

"Like I care what you believe," Mikey said.

"Well," Louis said. "Well. If you're so great, Mee-Shell —"

Mikey did stand up then. Louis didn't back away.

"Go ahead, Mee-Shell. Try it. You'll get yourself suspended if you start a fight in the classroom. And good riddance."

"She's not starting it, Louie," Ronnie said. "You are."

"No I'm not. And you better button it, Ron."

"Who made *you* king?" Mikey demanded.

"We'll see who's the one who's lying," Louis said. "I'll bring the biscuits tomorrow." When Louis got angry, his whole face turned pink. "This is all your stupid fault, Ronnie."

"Leave Ronnie out of this," Mikey told him.

Outside, after lunch, during noon recess, Margalo tried to find out from Mikey. "Do you really? Have you eaten dog biscuits?"

Mikey was hurrying towards the soccer game. "Come on."

Margalo hung back. She tried to explain — "I don't like sports. I never did, not even in first grade and I liked everything about school in first grade. Especially sports in teams."

"Do it to show the boys. Why should they get that field to themselves, and be the ones who tell everybody what teams? As if they were so great. I bet I'm the best soccer player here."

"I believe you, but —"

"They just always think they should have things all their own way. How bad can a dog biscuit be?"

"So you never did before?"

"I never had a dog. What would I be doing with dog biscuits?" Mikey asked.

"So you were lying?"

"I'm not going to let him get away with thinking he's so great," Mikey said. "Are you going to play?"

"I'll watch," Margalo said.

"Maybe you're better than you think."

Margalo shook her head.

"Anyway," Mikey gave up, "it's Tanisha I really want to have play. She moves like a good athlete. As if she'd be fast. If you're afraid," Mikey looked right at Margalo, "or embarrassed," she added and smiled a quarrelsome *Can-you-take-the-truth?* smile.

Margalo stared right back at Mikey's face, and didn't say a word. Not. One. Word. Mikey shrugged her shoulders and turned away, running towards the soccer field. She was disappointed in Margalo.

Margalo stood still for a minute. Who did Mikey Elsinger think she was, anyway? Then the Gap girls joined her.

Margalo called them the Gap girls because they

always dressed in Gap clothes, Gap jeans and Gap shirts, Gap skirts, Gap cotton sweaters, Gap-pastel-colored socks. They dressed alike and wore their hair alike, at Lois Lane length with bangs, except for Rhonda Ransom, who had beautiful, long, almost white blonde hair that she wore pulled back from her face with a headband.

Even Mikey had to admit that Rhonda had the prettiest hair in the class, and Mikey said the Gap girls bored her stupid, Rhonda and Sharon and Karen, with Lindsey hanging around the edges trying so hard to belong that Margalo wanted to kick her in the shins. "What pet are you going to bring?" Sharon asked Margalo. "I'm bringing my dog, it's a Lhasa, imported from Tibet."

The Gap girls almost always handed Margalo a laugh. She didn't know why they were interested in her, except she was new and her hair was — temporarily — the right length. They had to know she wasn't like them. She told them, the first time they came up to her to make friendly, that Blossom made her want to throw up. They, of course, thought Blossom was cool, and perfect, and beautiful, and brilliant. "She's my hero," they said.

Karen asked Margalo, "Do you have a dog? My dog just had puppies, and you could have one of those. They're beagles and they're really cute."

"I'd love a puppy," Lindsey said. "I always wanted a puppy."

"I don't know," Karen said. "My parents would have to give permission. And you'd have to pay."

"I'll ask my mother."

"They might all be gone already," Karen warned.

"I'm bringing my budgie," Rhonda said. "Noah will probably bring some frog, like he did last year, and Louis will bring his horrible dog. Is Mikey really going to eat a dog biscuit?"

"She said she was," Margalo reminded them.

"I know," Rhonda confided. "But I thought you might know, if — if she was just — saying that?"

"How would I know?" Margalo asked.

"Because you're her friend," Rhonda said.

Margalo asked Mikey about that, later, as they were packing up their backpacks at the end of school, "Am I your friend?"

Mikey was surprised by the question. "Why? Do you want to be?"

"No, I mean, are we friends?" Margalo asked.

"Not yet," Mikey said. She smiled a stingy smile, and asked, "Were you counting on it?"

Margalo turned away, again, and walked away, again, and Mikey —

Mikey knew before she opened her mouth that she shouldn't say what she was about to say. She didn't know why she had said it, except she didn't want Margalo thinking that Mikey was counting on having her for a friend. As if Mikey needed friends.

Mikey didn't blame Margalo a bit for walking away.

But she didn't know what she could do about it. She couldn't unsay what she'd said.

And she didn't have a pet. She'd never had one. Not even a goldfish.

"My father said once he'd get me a gerbil. But I wanted a dog," Mikey was telling Margalo. "If I know what I really want, do you think I ought to say something else is good enough?" It was already Tuesday. She could always be sick, and stay home from school on Pet Day.

As usual, in the morning it felt as if the night had flattened out all the things she regretted from the day before, and made them even with the rest of things, like a black marble rolling pin rolling yesterday out like a pie crust. So the new day felt entirely new.

Margalo seemed to feel the same way. New day, new start. No grudges. "I'm thinking of bringing in one of the little kids' gerbils," she said. "They have cages, and my mom can't get down to school to bring me any of the cats. We're a cat family, more than gerbils. Right now we've got eight because of the kittens, but really there are only three. Do you want a kitten? Or they might have to go to the pound. Which is better than being abandoned, and running wild. At least everyone says it's better. I'd rather run wild, wouldn't you? There's an all-black one but it's a male; but you could have that one and we could name it Beelzebub."

"I can't."

"Well, I'm sorry because it would have been fun. If Mom could, she'd bring the kittens in — but she doesn't have the car, and anyway she has the babies at home. They're too young to be left alone. But she says if I could get them here she bets we'd get rid of all of them. The kittens, not the babies. Are you really going to eat a dog biscuit?"

"If Louis can I can. I didn't know this town had a pound."

"That or an animal shelter. Places usually have them. We usually have kittens so we need to know about the animal shelters."

"Why don't you have the mother spayed?"

"We can't afford things like that," Margalo said.

"Isn't it cheaper than feeding kittens?"

"She feeds them."

"They'll just be put down, you know that, don't you? That's what happens to most of the animals that go to a shelter."

"That's not true."

"Yes it is. It's a known fact."

"That's not necessarily true."

"It's irresponsible not to have her spayed."

Margalo stared at Mikey and didn't say anything.

Mikey thought maybe Margalo wanted to talk about something else. "So what's this gerbil's name you're bringing?" She hoped it was a friendly smile she was putting on her face. She couldn't be sure; she didn't have much practice with friendly smiles.

Then she had an idea. "Maybe," she said, before Margalo could even start to answer the question, "I could bring in a roadkill. You know? In a shoe box, and I could make holes in the side of the box, with a pencil or the points of scissors."

"That's really barfmaking," Margalo said and her face lit up. "They'd scream their heads off. I bet, don't you think? I mean, they'd really scream, all the girls, especially the Gap girls, I bet."

"*You* wouldn't," Mikey said. She was glad to say something that would make Margalo feel good. She guessed maybe she wouldn't mind if Margalo did want to be friends.

"No. But I'd already know it's already dead. When something's already dead, the horrible part is all over with."

Mikey was relieved to hear that. She wondered if Margalo had seen a dead person.

"You can't hurt a dead body," Margalo said. "It's true," she said.

Mikey had another flash of idea. "You want to be a vet."

"How did you know?"

"I just knew."

"Anyway, it costs too much money to go to vet school."

"Maybe you can get loans, or scholarships."

"*Are* we friends?" Margalo asked, again. Nobody had ever guessed her vet dreams before. Not anybody.

"Why do you keep asking?"

"I don't know, why are you going to eat some stupid dog biscuit?"

"Who says it's stupid?"

"I do. Because it is."

"What do you know about anything?"

"I know enough to figure out when something is *that* stupid!"

Mikey whispered then, so low that her voice could barely be heard, "Then why are you yelling?" and she smiled a *Look-nice* smile.

And she ate the dog biscuit, too. She'd thought about whether she could really do it, and she'd thought that probably the biscuit would be hard, and tasteless, but not really bad if she didn't think about it. So when Louis strutted over and held out a Great Dane-sized, dog-bone-shaped biscuit to her, she didn't even think about it. She took a bite off one of the ends, and chewed, showing everyone how this wasn't any kind of a big deal. She swallowed. There was nothing much to it.

Louis looked like a jerk. *Jerk* was written all over his face. And that served him right, boasting about something that was such a big nothing. Mikey smiled a smirky smile, bit off another chunk, and chewed. She felt like a baseball pitcher on TV, chewing away while everyone watched. She kept her eye on Louis, showing him what a big nothing his big deal was. Then she offered a bite of the dog biscuit to Margalo. She wanted to share the glory with Margalo.

Margalo shook her head.

Mikey offered it again.

"No thanks."

"No, come on. It's nothing," Mikey promised.

"But why would I *want* to eat a dog biscuit?" Margalo asked.

Mikey's cheeks flamed, and she was so embarrased she could only hit back. "Chicken."

"I've decided what pet I'm bringing," Mikey announced to anyone near enough to hear.

Margalo, being in the next desk, was near enough. Mrs. Chemsky had gone to the office, to look in her mailbox. Mikey wasn't giving Margalo a chance to go on being enemies, if that was what

Margalo wanted. Mikey hoped that wasn't what Margalo wanted, and she didn't want to find out that it was. If it was.

Mikey wasn't sure you could make fresh starts two days in a row.

"I'm going to bring my mother," Mikey announced to anyone near enough to hear.

"Bummer."

"Great."

"On a leash?"

"My mother would never let me put *her* on a leash."

Mikey told them, "She'll only be here an hour, because she's too big to keep in a cage."

"Cool," seemed to be the opinion of the class, and Mikey was grinning away with her *I'm-one-of-a-kind* grin, and she caught Margalo giggling. She saw that, at the edge of her peripheral vision.

So everything was OK again.

Louis said, "I bet she's too big for a cage. If she's at all like you."

Mikey wasn't about to let that remark pass. "Meaning what?" she said, stalking over across the room.

But she knew what he meant, and everybody knew, which was why things got sort of quiet.

"Meaning, she's probably not an overly underweight person," Louis said, sarcastic.

He stood up, so Mikey couldn't lean over him at his desk.

"So now you're going to try name-calling?" Mikey demanded. "Like what? You know, if you start calling me names all that'll happen is you'll look like a wimp."

She turned her back on him and stalked away, but after only one and a half steps she stopped. She wheeled around. She said, "That is, even more of a wimp than usual." His face was turning pink.

She turned and stalked another one and a half steps.

Louis was just behind her, grabbing for her braid. But he missed because Mikey had stopped. She wheeled around again.

"And then I'd just have to start calling *you* names," she said. "Like Lunchface, or Gopher. Barfbag." She turned her back and took another step away. Spun back. "Snotfoot."

People were sort of laughing, and at Louis.

He grabbed Mikey's braid and pulled back hard. "What're you running away from, Mee-Shell?"

"Don't you touch my hair," Mikey said, and she punched him in the nose.

As Mrs. Chemsky came back to the room.

Louis howled in alarm, then jammed the heel of his hand up against his bleeding nose and was furiously silent.

The class scurried to get into its desks.

"Whatever —?" Mrs. Chemsky asked.

Mikey said, "He pulled my hair."

"She bunched be!" Louis wiped the back of his hand against his bleeding nose.

"Both of you —" Mrs. Chemsky said.

Everybody waited for the end of that sentence.

"— behave yourselves. There will be no more of this hitting. There will be no more of this teasing. Do you understand me?"

"Yes, Mrs. Chemsky," two voices answered.

"Good. Now. Louis, go wash up, and come directly back." Mrs. Chemsky opened her roll book. "Keith Adams."

"Here," Keith Adams answered, quickly.

"So I still have a chance to be the first person in the class who gets sent to the office," Mikey muttered. Margalo smiled in response, so everything was all right again.

But she didn't risk asking again if Margalo wanted to join in the soccer game. Tanisha and Rhonda were included, with more grumbling from the boys. It turned out that Tanisha was really good, fast with her feet, and that Rhonda — surprising everyone — made an all right fullback. The team on which the three girls played creamed Louis Caselli's team.

With Mikey as high scorer.

"Not fair, you shouldn't all be on the same team," was the complaint.

Tanisha and Rhonda and Mikey looked at one another. Mikey could almost have thought Rhonda was an OK human being.

Before that could happen, Rhonda said she would play on the Casellis' team, to make things more even. "You come, too, Tanisha," Rhonda said. "Mikey's the best, so both of us should play against her."

Louis said, "Bad defense, that's all. I'm going to cover more of the backfield. That'll change things."

"You *wish*," Mikey muttered, so he could hear her.

At that time, Margalo was telling a bunch of girls — Ronnie and her friends; Ronnie was the center of an everchanging and shapeless group of girls — about her half-brother's gerbil, which she might bring to Pet Day. Everyone was working hard to be friendly, finding cute things about a gerbil. "Hamlet's a funny name, don't you think?" Ann asked Annaliese. "I mean nice funny."

"Gerbils make good pets," Denise told Margalo. "The way they're always doing something? You can watch them, like a TV?"

Margalo was often kept up at night by Hamlet running in rattling circles on his wheel, but she didn't say that. "He said I can borrow Hamlet if I want to, because he's too young to bring a live pet," she told them. "He's in the afternoon kindergarten class, because we registered so late he couldn't get into the morning class. Because we didn't move until after the wedding. My mother's wedding, I mean. Not mine."

"How many brothers do you have?"

"If he's your half-brother, that means your mother had another husband, isn't that right?"

"Do you have sisters?"

"Do you have any real brothers and sisters?"

"What about your real father?"

"Do you share a bedroom?"

Margalo asked Ann, "What's your cat's name?" When Ann answered "Pookie," Margalo *oohed* and *cuted* the way she was supposed to. More names were offered to her, then, as she'd hoped they would be. "Mine's Madonna, because of the way she — well, she keeps having kittens, even though when we named her it was because she looked like Madonna, you know? That 'who the hell cares' way," Ronnie said.

"Cool," Margalo said. *She* would never tell someone they ought to have their private pet spayed. "I like that."

"Fluffy, because she is."

"Ooh, cute."

"Ginger. Well, she's got spirit, she can be pretty mean."

"I hope it's a marmalade cat. Ginger's the perfect name for a marmalade cat." They were lapping this up.

"Can I tell you something?" Denise asked, her dark eyes sincere.

"Sure." Margalo got ready to hear something negative.

"We thought — we did, didn't we?" Denise's friends waited to hear what she would say before they agreed. "Well we did, we sort of thought you were, not exactly, but sort of, a little stuck-up? As if we weren't as interesting as other people?"

Margalo wrinkled her eyebrows, and she was sorry they might have thought that; except it was sort of true. If she was being completely honest, she'd have to admit she didn't find them all that interesting compared to Mikey. Except Ronnie, she thought; maybe. "But why?" she asked.

"We just met you. We don't know you at all," Ann said.

"You're always hanging around with Mikey," Derrie added. Derrie had curly red hair and wore gold hoops in her ears. She also talked through her nose, in a way that made her sound cynical and sophisticated, even when what she was saying wasn't.

"You mean Michelle, don't you?" Ronnie laughed, and others joined in.

Margalo wanted to tell them that she liked Mikey. Mikey was more interesting than most people, she wanted to tell them; although they were all very nice, it wasn't that, she added in her mind. "We sit next to each other," she pointed out.

"So do I sit next to you," Annaliese pointed out.

"Anyway," Margalo said before this conversation could go any further, "there's something I want to know. If you might know. Because you've all been here at WSE, and you might have heard. Except you, Derrie," she said, "but I wanted to ask you all if it was true about Mrs. Chemsky. That she's a witch."

First, they laughed, as if it was a joke.

"I don't have to be an old student to know *that*," Derrie said.

"You know?" Ann Tarwell said. "Justin says the boys all hate her, too."

"But I don't hate her," Margalo said. "I just wondered. Because it was something I heard, somewhere, I can't remember. I have such a bad memory, I can't remember who, or when, but I thought somebody said, that Mrs. Chemsky is a witch. I mean, a real one, who studies magic. Spells, and herbs, rituals. . . . Don't you know about those? The goddess worship, which is a really old religion?"

They didn't, and she knew it. She didn't, either, but they didn't know that.

"What kind of spells? You mean, like love potions?"

"I don't know," Margalo said, and that at least was true. "I just was asking. Do you think your cats will get into fights on Pet Day?" she said. "With all those dogs around. How do you keep them from fighting, or from running away, don't you worry about them? On Pet Day," she said. She was in total charge of the conversation now.

"Fluffy hates crowds, so she always climbs up? into my lap?"

"That must be so cute," Margalo said. She came from a big family so she knew how to get along with people by going along. "I always wanted a dog," she told them, "but that would be too much trouble with how big my family keeps getting."

"Too bad," Doucelle said. Denise was the color of milk chocolate, but Doucelle had skin the color of Margalo's mother's morning coffee, a silky dark brown; and she wore bold African-print tunics that her mother, the art teacher, made. "We always have dogs in our house."

"We always have some kind of pet," Annaliese said, "if you count fish. Do you count fish?"

"I would," Margalo said. "And I do have a whole lot of brothers and sisters," she reminded them. "So it's almost as good as pets," Margalo said. She knew approximately what they were thinking, and she looked over to the soccer game, pretending to pay attention to something else. They were thinking approximately exactly what she wanted them to think.

On the field, Mikey charged right up to tackle Harvey Smith and Lee Cheung, but they were too quick for her. At least, that was what it looked like. The two boys waited until the last minute and then Lee passed the ball behind Mikey, and Harvey was ready and he trapped it, then — because Mikey had wheeled around — he passed it backwards, to Lee.

This all happened fast, so fast that Margalo couldn't see how Mikey could keep turning around so fast, and running, too.

Mikey couldn't, of course. She lost her footing, and stumbled. As he ran by her, Louis reached down to jerk at her braid.

Mikey didn't even try to follow the ball and intercept Lee's goal shot. She ran after Louis and kicked him in his right leg, on the calf, without any warning and from behind.

Margalo smiled, and she turned around to look at Ronnie and her friends. They were perfectly nice girls and perfectly ordinary. She didn't have anything against them. They were trying to be friendly and she knew that she probably wanted them to think she was an OK person.

She wanted them to consider her a friend. She liked Derrie's red hair and Doucelle's proud face, and Ronnie had a not-girly look to her. But Margalo had to tell them, "I sort of like Mikey."

Ann shrugged, and turned to Ronnie, then the others. "Well, sure," she said.

"It's none of our business," Ronnie said.

Margalo nodded. She wondered how they'd take it if she told them she'd made it up about Mrs. Chemsky being a witch.

"It's a free country," Derrie said.

"Everyone's entitled to her own opinion," they agreed.

"That's what I think," Margalo said.

She thought, somehow, that Mikey would be friendly to her, after that. But Mikey ignored her most of that day. They didn't talk, or write notes, or anything. Mrs. Chemsky didn't yell at them even once.

On Thursday, Mikey didn't say anything about what pet she might bring, until Annaliese finally asked her, across Margalo's desk, "Have you decided what your pet will be?"

"Of course," Mikey said. She didn't look up from the book she was pretending to read, which was *The Wind in the Willows*.

"And?" Annaliese asked.

"You'll see," Mikey said, and turned a page.

"Why won't you say?" Annaliese asked.

"Because Porky's not bringing anything. Can't you figure that out?" Louis asked.

"Because she's a fake," said his sidekick Justin.

Mikey read on.

"She used to have pets," Louis said. "But — how do you think anyone gets that round? What do you think she's been eating? I don't think she has any pets left to bring. She's wearing them all."

They seemed to think that was pretty funny.

Mikey snapped her book closed "You can all just wait. Let it be a surprise," she said, a *You-are-such-twerps* smile all over her face. "It'll be worth the wait," she promised them. "Won't it, Margalo?"

Margalo didn't hesitate. "You bet," she said, as if she knew what Mikey was talking about, and she wasn't going to tell, either. As if they really were friends.

Mrs. Chemsky had predicted a fair and warm Pet Day, and her class was not surprised when her prediction came true. They had been watching the teacher carefully. As Pet Day had approached, the class noticed that Mrs. Chemsky seemed uneasy, which they attributed to pre-Pet Day anxiety. After all, what if she had to act heroically again? Also, they knew teachers were made nervous by parents coming onto the scene, disrupting the balance of power. But if Mrs. Chemsky was a witch, they reasoned, no one — not even a parent — could do her much damage, and certainly no animal could hurt her.

Mrs. Chemsky even told them, as if it was criticism not praise, that she had never had a class become so well-behaved so early in the year, and with Pet Day approaching. She hoped they weren't anxious about their pets coming to school. She could promise them that in all the years she had been teaching, all pets had been popular. For weren't all animals, like all people, different? and each lovable in its own way? She hoped their exemplary behavior had to do with their good intentions, she told them.

The class had nodded their heads and then remembered to say, "Yes, Mrs. Chemsky." If she was a witch, and had unnatural powers, they didn't want to offend her. They hoped their pets wouldn't cause any trouble.

On Friday morning, most of the fifth-grade pets were not present. Five gerbils dozed in two habitat cages on the deep windowsills, watched by Rhonda's budgerigar. Two small fishbowls with bright tropical fish swimming in them were safe on Mrs. Chemsky's desk. Several of the children were going to be petless this year but others expected more than a dozen dogs, cats, and rabbits to arrive

in time for the parade. Veronica Caselli's mother —
if it wasn't one thing it was another — was bringing
in a ferret. Mrs. Chemsky had made clear to Veronica her strong suspicion that this was a ferret
belonging to Someone Else, perhaps some Older
Caselli cousin. Veronica denied the charge passion-
ately, although she had offered with unexpected
reasonableness to leave the ferret home if that was
what Mrs. Chemsky wanted. Uneasily, Mrs. Chemsky declined the offer.

Margalo arrived on Pet Day carrying a small cage
made out of wire mesh; its handle was a twisted
rope. She set it down on her desktop, then slid into
the seat.

Girls' voices squealed, alarmed, and those who
had gathered to greet Margalo backed away. Several
of the boys came closer.

"A rat?"

"Is that a rat?"

"But it's not white. Is that a wild rat?"

"Oh, wow."

Word spread.

"Just a rodent, like a gerbil, only bigger. What's
the problem with you chickens?"

"It's that horrible gray real rats are. And its tail,
too."

"Cool."

"Why would she?"

"Really cool."

"How could she?"

"Where'd you get it, Margalo?"

"One of my stepbrothers trapped it. At the dump. Sometimes the high school kids go to the dump, looking for car parts and things. To fix up their cars and things with. You know. But," Margalo added, pleased with her success, "you better not stick your fingers into its cage. Because you can never tell with wild animals. If they might have rabies."

The children backed away as Mrs. Chemsky made a slow approach to Margalo's desk.

"She has to send it home," Derrie announced.

"I love all rodents," Harvey Smith maintained, and he punched Malcolm Johnson on the arm. "Yeah, man," Malcolm agreed, and knuckled Harvey happily.

"Some people eat rats," Louis announced. This news was greeted with a chorus of groans and gaggings. "Ask Lee. It's true, isn't it, Lee?"

But Louis could never rattle Lee, who answered just the question he was asked. "I never did, but I've heard of it. It would be a good way to control the rat problem in cities, wouldn't it?"

"Not Hamlet," Margalo maintained. "Nobody's eating Hamlet."

"I thought," Mrs. Chemsky said, "that you told us Hamlet was a gerbil."

"Did I?" Margalo said. "My stepbrother names everything Hamlet. Even my mom's car, he calls that Hamlet, too. Because it has a tragic life. We don't even know if this is a boy rat or a girl one, but he named it Hamlet anyway."

Mrs. Chemsky stayed calm, and in control. "Hamlet certainly seems to have caused a stir. Would you like to set him on the window with the others?"

"She should take it home, Mrs. Chemsky. Wild isn't a pet. Is it? Or you could make it die? Can't you? Puh-lease?"

"Good heavens, Denise. How would I do that? And why should I, when it's safe in a cage?"

"I made the cage myself," Margalo announced.

People backed still farther away, even Harvey and Malcolm.

At that point Mikey came in. She was carrying a shoe box, with holes punched in it. Mrs. Chemsky had both of her hands on the rope handle of Hamlet's cage, about to lift it and carry it to a windowsill. Mikey pushed her way through to her own desk. She set her shoe box down on it. "Don't anybody touch this. It's dangerous."

"I can't stand this!" Karen Blackaway cried, and she went to her own desk where she climbed up onto the seat, and sat down on the writing surface, with her feet safely off the floor. "Pet Day is supposed to be fun," she reminded Mrs. Chemsky, as if this was all Mrs. Chemsky's fault.

"I'm having fun," Sal Caselli said. "Aren't you, Louis?"

Mrs. Chemsky had just about lifted the rat's cage up. She was holding it awkwardly, because the rat was running around inside.

"Don't touch him, Mrs. Chemsky," Margalo said. "Be careful!"

"Just hold it by the handle," Noah advised.

"I said," Mikey said in a low, warning voice, "stay away."

"I heard you," Louis Caselli answered, and his hand flew out. This knocked the shoe box off her desk.

The top flew off the box and landed two feet away.

"Oops," Louis said.

More people climbed up onto seats, not even waiting to get back to their own desks.

Gravel, and clumped grass-and-twigs fell out of the shoe box, and a couple of handfuls of leaves.

Some girls screamed in little oooohs, some whimpered, and some of the boys squealed, too, although they tried to pretend that they were the boys who were swearing.

Mrs. Chemsky jerked around, to see what was the matter.

The handle to Hamlet's cage came undone. The cage hung down by the rope end. Then, that knot untied itself and the cage dropped onto the floor.

More people rushed over to the desks and stood on them.

Henry Weisler's desk fell over, sideways, and lay there. Its feet stuck out straight, like rigor mortis. Henry scrambled up from where he'd fallen onto his back, and ran to the hall door.

Two other desks crashed down over onto the floor.

"You stupid —!" and Mikey punched Louis in the chest.

"It's your fault, Porky," he told her. He grabbed at her arm. A rope burn was what she deserved, and he'd be happy to give it to her.

"What was that? Miss Elsinger, I'm talking to you," Mrs. Chemsky called out, over the confusion of voices.

"A shoe box," Mikey told the teacher.

"Probably there wasn't anything in it," Derrie suggested, sounding bored although she was sitting at her desk with her knees drawn up against her chest.

"Who says?" Mikey demanded. She looked all around her, her eyes bright as she jerked her arm away from Louis.

"You probably don't even have a pet."

"Yeah, because no pet would stay. He'd run away. Or you'd eat him," Louis said, and gave up trying to give her a rope burn. Trying for a rope burn meant he was in range for a punch. But if he could wait until the teacher looked away, get behind her and pull on her braid, pull really hard, jerking her head around — that was what *really* got her going.

"People say, I've heard," Lee Cheung offered into the conversation, "that rats taste like wild ducks."

"Miss Elsinger?" Mrs. Chemsky raised her voice to Serious Warning.

"May I please be excused?" Hadrian Klenk asked from the doorway. He was standing with one hand raised.

The teacher didn't pay any attention to him.

"You'd better say, Mikey," Margalo advised.

Margalo's eyes were sparkling, like she knew some big secret. Mikey couldn't figure it out, unless Margalo was trying to make her look stupid, or trying to get her into trouble.

Then Mikey saw what nobody else — except probably Margalo — had noticed yet.

"I better say what?" Mikey asked.

"What you told me yesterday," Margalo said. "About bringing a black widow spider for Pet Day."

Two more desks fell over, and Rhonda was crying, because she said her wrist hurt. "Maybe I broke it," she said.

"All right, class," Mrs. Chemsky said. "Everything is all right. Your wrist is fine, Rhonda. Hadrian, you will have to wait to be excused. Let's everyone get back to — who opened that cage?"

"There's the rat!" screamed Lindsey. "I see it!"

Three more desks fell over.

"There!"

"There!"

"Now, everyone — class? Stand still. Remember, he is more frightened of you than you are of him."

"Not me. I'm a lot more frightened of him."

"Stand still," Mrs. Chemsky said, her voice very calm, now. "Or sit quietly." She followed her own advice, sitting on her desk chair, and gathering her knees up to her chest.

One advantage of having a strict teacher, who you suspect might be a witch, is that you can feel safe with her. The class hurriedly picked up desks, "There he goes!", and sat down in them, "If someone opens the cloakroom door, you could chase him out, couldn't you, Mrs. Chemsky?", with feet up.

"It's all *your* fault, Margalo. *You* chase him," Rhonda said.

Margalo stared at her, expressionless.

Hadrian Klenk still had his hand up in the air. "May I please be excused?" he asked.

"Not just now, Hadrian. Margalo is going to open

the cloakroom door. Hamlet would undoubtedly prefer being outside to being inside with us."

"I would," Louis joked. "I do."

Without looking at all nervous, Margalo set her feet down on the ground. She walked between the desks as if there were no wild rat loose in the room, and no black widow spider to worry about, either.

In fact, there was no black widow spider, as she knew, since she had made that up.

And the rat, she had seen, was hiding behind the bookcase by Mrs. Chemsky's desk.

Margalo walked calmly over and opened the door that led from the cloakroom to the outside. Then she walked calmly back and sat down, and drew her knees up against her chest.

"Now what?" Ira asked. "Now what do we do? Are we going to go on sitting here?"

Mikey was watching Margalo carefully. No matter what, Margalo was brave, braver than any of the rest of them, and a good liar, too. A really good liar and pretty sneaky, too, a sneaky, tricky person. Mikey thought, she wouldn't mind at all being friends with Margalo.

"I think Hamlet is frightened of us," Margalo said. "But I have a suggestion. If we all go outside, I bet he'd run out when it was empty in here."

"I have to admit," Mrs. Chemsky reluctantly admitted, getting reluctantly back down from her perch, "that may be the most efficient way to get rid of the rat. I hope your brother will understand how Hamlet came to be lost," she said, sounding like she hoped the opposite. "Let us go quietly, class. Outside. Slowly," she advised, but nobody could hear her. Mrs. Chemsky moved slowly anyway. It was only 8:50.

"What about my spider?" Mikey asked.

The stampede increased.

"If I see it, I'll kill it for you, Pork-o," Louis offered.

"Jerk," Mikey answered.

"If I see it, I'll believe it," Rhonda said, which was the first intelligent thing she had said that year.

"All of you, outside," Mrs. Chemsky said. She told them she couldn't leave the room until it was empty of students, as if the building were on fire, or a ship sinking in the ocean. She announced that she would watch the door from outside, until the rat left the building. She would leave a trail of crumbled chocolate chip cookies — cookies she had baked last night and brought for her own morning snack, and now had to give up for this rat — to the cloakroom door.

Mrs. Chemsky did not allow her class to take part in the Parade of Pets. They were kept inside to do the language arts work they were supposed to have accomplished during the first hour of school. The parents who were going to bring in the larger and the uncaged pets had to be telephoned by their children, to be told that there was no need to come to school with the dogs, and cats, and rabbits, or the Caselli ferret, either.

One at a time, the children were excused from the class to call their parents, in strict alphabetical order.

3

Driving Louis Caselli Crazy

"I hate him," Mikey said. Across the playground, Louis Caselli had grabbed some little second-grader by the shoulder, to shake loose the soccer ball the kid was clutching to his chest.

Mikey and Margalo, like most of the rest of the school, were staying outside in the sunshine until the second bell rang. Louis picked up the soccer ball and started strutting over.

"I'd like to punch him so hard his nose comes out the back of his head," Mikey said.

"Can you do that?" Margalo wondered. "Not you, not you personally and Louis, I mean. I mean, can someone really hit someone that hard? Wouldn't the nose come out back end first? Would it be able to keep its shape, aren't there bones? Even not counting the skull."

"Of course you can't. But you can kill somebody with a good nose punch." Mikey smiled her level-three mean smile at Louis, *You-lose-you-loser.*

He smiled right back, but he didn't have her meanness skills. "Morning, Mee-Shell."

Mikey clenched her fists.

"Oops, sorry, forgot," Louis smirked. Some of his friends were following, to see what would happen. "I mean, Morning, Porky," Louis said. "Oops, sorry again, I'm not supposed to call you that either, am I?" He grinned around at his friends.

Margalo couldn't think of what to say. She wanted to think of something to say that would make Louis afraid to pick a fight with Mikey, but she couldn't think what that might be.

Mikey took a punch at Louis but he was ready for her and blocked it. He grabbed her braid and jerked down on it. "Nice try, Blimpo. But you missed. Missed by a mile."

"I'm not," Mikey said, "fat. I'm solid."

"Yeah, right, solid. Solid fat," Louis said.

"You are going to get in big trouble, Louis Caselli," Margalo said.

He backed off, hands in the air. "Oh, wow.

Thanks for warning me, Margalo. Save me, guys, I'm going to get in big trouble."

They all went off, laughing.

"I really," Mikey said, and she was stiff with anger, her hands still in fists. "Hate," she said, and punched her knuckles together so hard Margalo thought it must really hurt. "Him."

"He's worse to you than anyone else," Margalo said.

"Worse? Worse is what he is on a good day," Mikey said.

"He can make Rhonda cry," Margalo said, thinking. In a way, she was relieved that Louis Caselli mostly ignored her. But in another way she was insulted. She wondered how she'd do, up against Louis Caselli. "And he chases Hadrian to make fun of the way he runs." Being super smart at everything didn't help Hadrian much with Louis, either. "I just can't figure out why Louis picks on you."

"He doesn't," Mikey answered. "He can't pick on me. But he sure would like to. He sure tries to," Mikey said. "If I thought that — idiot cousin of an Australian trotweiler — could even come close to picking on me, I'd . . . I'd shoot myself."

"You're the only one who tells him to his face what a jerk he is," Margalo said.

"Or I'd shoot him."

The bell rang, buzzing in the warm air.

"I'd rather shoot him," Mikey said. "Or I'd hire Mrs. Chemsky — a well-known witch — to cast a spell on him. A bad one, the kind where he would *wish* he'd only been turned into a frog."

"What do you mean, a witch?" Margalo asked, hurrying to keep up.

"Everybody knows about Mrs. Chemsky. You must have heard it. I can't even remember who told me. Now what?" she demanded, because Margalo was going nuts, right there twenty-five feet from the classroom door. Margalo was clapping her hands together and stamping her feet on the ground.

"Listen. Listen to this. I made it up," Margalo gasped. "I — made — that — up."

"Made what up? Never mind, I'm not waiting for you any longer."

They halted by their cubbies.

"Tell me now," Mikey said, opening her backpack to take out the books and lunch box.

Margalo looked around, then whispered. "I made that up. I did. About Mrs. Chemsky. About her being a witch. And now, see? Everybody believes it. And I started it." They moved over to their desks. "So," Margalo said in a low voice, between saying "Hey" to Tanisha and "Hey" to Ann, and Derrie, Lynn, Ira, who all called "Hey, Margalo." Margalo said, "So," in a low voice, her words hidden among all of the voices saying hello at the start of the day.

"So, so? So, what?" Mikey asked.

"So I'm having an idea. I'll tell you about it at recess. If I'm through thinking by then," Margalo said, just smiling away like somebody had made her queen.

Mikey smiled right back, the *We're-about-to-make-some-trouble* smile that always made her feel so good.

At morning recess, Margalo pulled Mikey around to the front playground, for privacy. "We need to know who his girlfriend is."

"Louis Caselli has a girlfriend?"

"I don't know. But there's probably someone he likes. Or says he likes, wants people to think he likes. Ronnie might know."

"She won't tell us. Who cares, anyway?"

"Because," and Margalo's eyes were practically dancing in her face. If her eyes had had feet, they would have been doing crisscross hip-hopping dancing right there on either side of her nose. "The more we know, the more ways we can get at him. And get back at him. And drive him crazy."

"Who'd like him anyway?" Mikey wanted to know.

"I think, some girls sort of do. He's sort of a class leader."

"I don't believe either one of that."

"Anyway, Ronnie'll know," Margalo said.

"That's not leadership. It's bullyship."

"Because they're cousins, and they live on the same street, practically next door, and they play together practically every day, after school. They always did, because their fathers are brothers, but Sal's is the only mother who doesn't have a job. They're nurses. The other mothers."

"You're making this up."

"Ronnie was talking."

"Telling you who she hangs with after school?"

"No, of course not. Don't you ever listen to someone and learn more than just what they're saying?"

Mikey tried to recall. "I don't think so. I have a hard enough time just figuring out what people mean."

"That's because you're so self-involved," Margalo explained, but not as if it was a criticism.

But how could that not be a criticism?

"That's one of the main things about you," Margalo said. "You don't pretend to be nice, or unselfish."

"But I'm not unselfish," Mikey pointed out. She was surprised, and pleased, too, that Margalo understood that about her. "And I'm not nice, so why should I pretend?"

"I know, but —. Anyway," Margalo said, changing the subject. Because she *did* pretend. "We're talking about Louis, and who his girlfriend is."

"I don't believe he has one. Can you imagine? Kissing Louis Caselli?"

They groaned, and they moaned, and they gagged.

"But you know," Margalo said, "in a book, you two would end up together, you and Louis Caselli, boyfriend and girlfriend. Do you think you will?"

"Ask me why I don't read books," Mikey said. "C'mon, ask."

During lunch recess, Margalo joined Ronnie and her friends. They were deciding what they wanted to do — four-square, dodgeball, jump rope — standing around, talking about it, not making any decisions. The girls wore shorts, or jeans, so Margalo fit right in, now that the first day of school was over. Margalo had a big supply of hand-me-down shirts from her older stepbrothers and she wore about the same thing to school every day, jeans or shorts and a long-sleeved button-down shirt, not tucked in, with the sleeves rolled up to her elbows. They thought she looked cool and she agreed with them. She kind of liked most of these girls. They were *Star Trek: The Next Generation* fans.

For a while, Margalo just listened, and watched

the soccer game. "Did you see, last night . . . ?"
"There was this sweater I almost talked Mom into
getting for me. . . ." "My horrible little brother, and
his horrible little friend. . . ."

Over on the soccer field, Mikey trapped the ball,
and passed it ahead to Tanisha, then Mikey charged
ahead to pick up the pass Tanisha sent on to her.
Nobody could stop them. They had made a fast
break. Louis was in the goal, moving from side to
side, trying to see past his fullbacks, yelling at anyone who got in his line of sight until they turned
around to look at him, and then yelling at them to
pay attention to the game, stupid.

"Is Louis going to be this way all year? about
Mikey," Margalo asked Ronnie, sort of quietly.

Ronnie never beat around any bushes. She wore
her hair straight and short, and so were her answers
to questions. "Louis picks out someone every year,"
Ronnie said. "I mean, someone special. Last year it
was Lynnie, I don't know why, it isn't as if she asked
for it like Mikey does, or was weird like Hadrian is,
and the funny thing is that this year he's got a crush
on her. The year before that it was Rhonda. He says
Rhonda's his favorite because he likes the way she
snivels."

Sometimes, Margalo had to agree with Louis.
"Isn't it ever anyone popular?"

"He picked on Ira for a while last year. Because he

was new and his ears stick out. Louis likes to find people with something wrong with them."

"How can you stand him?"

Ronnie shrugged. "He's my cousin. I like Sal better, personally, but — when someone's your cousin he's your cousin. Louis isn't so bad if you don't let him — look. There she goes again — she's really good."

Mikey had faked a pass. Louis had moved across the goal cage in response to the fake. But she kept the ball and took the shot. Louis saw it, reversed, and stumbled, recovered his balance, but by then two fullbacks had moved between him and Mikey, so when the ball came in he couldn't see it. Or block it.

Mikey's team crowded around her, slapping palms. "One more for the good guys. We are *on* today, on a roll."

Louis was cussing out his teammates, and pushing at them, until they pushed back. That fight never got going, however, because people wanted to play soccer more than they wanted to quarrel about whose fault it was that Mikey had scored another point.

Margalo almost laughed out loud. Some days ideas just poured out of her like water boiling up over the edge of the pot and spattering onto the stovetop. "You know," she said, loud enough so everyone around could hear, "it's not fair to have just boys on the soccer team. The boys aren't that much better than the girls and some girls they're nowhere near as good as, don't you think?"

"Don't you think at least Mikey and Tanisha are good enough to play on the team?" Annaliese asked.

"Rhonda, too. Rhonda's an OK soccer player."

"It's not even legal, you know," Margalo said. "When girls can't play on the team. It's discrimination against sex. No, that's not what I mean, you know what I mean, you don't all have to laugh at me. I'm right, it *is* discrimination."

"But none of the schools we play have mixed teams."

"And that's not legal, either. I bet."

"We should do something about that."

"Why would I want to play on a team with those creeps?" Mikey demanded.

"It's not fair that you don't have the chance to," Ronnie and Derrie said. "For the school," they said.

Mikey didn't care about the school. "I've only been here two weeks." But she didn't mind being popular.

"Don't you care if our team wins?"

Mikey made an end run around that question. "Tanisha? What do you think? You wanna?"

Tanisha shrugged. "They won't like it, if we ask.

And if Coach lets us they'll like it even less. But — hey — a girl's gotta try, right? Otherwise nothing ever changes."

"What about you, Rhonda?" they asked.

"Well," Rhonda hesitated. "It's not fair, you're right, but. . . ." Rhonda had changed back into her skirt, changing out of the shorts she changed into at recess so she could play soccer. "Do you want me to ask Mrs. Chemsky if we can ask Mr. Delaney?"

They knew there was no way of stopping Rhonda from doing something, if it made her feel important. Mikey figured the decision was now out of her hands. She wouldn't mind playing real games, now she thought of it; and she wouldn't mind having some real coaching, either. Especially she wouldn't mind at all if she could get even better at soccer. *ME*, she wrote, at the top of her math worksheet. Then she raised her hand for permission to sharpen her pencil, because she'd forgotten to do that after recess.

Mrs. Chemsky didn't like being interrupted in the middle of directions, but she was fair. That was the bad thing about Mrs. Chemsky. She wanted to be fair and she was also a pretty good teacher. That made it hard on her class.

As she returned to her seat with her sharpened pencil, Mikey read the single word added under *Me* at the top of Margalo's paper. The word was: *Lynnie.*

It took her ten math problems to figure out what that meant.

She had to wait until the end of school, and the seven minutes between dismissal and their buses leaving, to ask what Margalo was going to do about Lynnie and Louis. "She can't like him back," Mikey decided.

"I can't imagine it," Margalo agreed. "You're going to play on the soccer team, aren't you?"

"Unless we aren't allowed."

"They'll have to let you, if you make a big enough stink, if he tries not to."

"I guess that's right. So I guess I will."

"Good."

"Why do you care?"

"I have an idea."

"What idea?"

"Tell you tomorrow."

But by tomorrow Mikey had forgotten Margalo had something to tell her, because the whole class was in an uproar, and the sixth grade, too, apparently, if the boys could be believed. "Girls on the soccer team?" "Who do they think they're kidding?" The boys were dumbfounded, shocked, appalled. They were furious. They were really mad. "What are you trying to do? You'll ruin the game!" "I'll quit the team." "We'll really lose now." "Nobody wants it. Everybody thinks it's wrong." "You don't know anything about a real game. There's *much* more pressure. It's entirely different."

"You'll be sorry. Mee-Shell," Louis said. "You're going to get hurt. You, too," he said to Tanisha. "And you," he told Rhonda.

"You're just afraid we'll do better than you," Rhonda said.

"You think that? Boy, do you need brain surgery."

"Oh, yeah?" Rhonda wondered.

"Oh, yeah," Louis answered.

"Who says?" Rhonda wondered.

"It's as clear as that zit on your chin," Louis said. Rhonda's hand covered her chin. "Do not."

"I'm not worried about you, you quit everything anyway," Louis said.

"Do not."

"Do, too. Everybody knows. You're a quitter. Q is your middle initial."

"No it isn't. It's E. For Elizabeth, my middle name."

"Like we all know you're a crybaby. Don't we?"

"Not anymore," Rhonda said, rubbing her nose. "You're mean, Louis Caselli," and she ran away to the girls' bathroom, calling over her shoulder, "You're really *mean*."

Mikey muttered, "Jerk."

"Who?" Margalo asked.

"Both of them." Mikey yelled after Rhonda,

"You're a pair of prize pea brains!" She turned to smile right at Louis Caselli, right in his face. "Both of you!" she yelled into his face.

Mrs. Chemsky entered the classroom then, and settled everyone down, and sat everyone down, and took attendance. That done, she had a serious announcement to make. She stood in front of them for a very long time, or what felt like a very long time. She looked each of the thirty-one students in the eye, one after the other. Afterwards, nobody was sure whether she'd looked them in the eye in alphabetical order, or not.

"I've received phone calls, at my home," Mrs. Chemsky announced, "after school hours, in the evening, and Mr. Delaney has had many more, both at home and at school, and I want to tell all of you now, loud and clear, that it's a senseless story that is going around about me being a witch. I don't know how it got started, but I insist that it stop. Right now. Right here. I am not a witch. I am a Congregationalist."

She waited, and watched them all.

Then she smiled a smile that wasn't strict, and it didn't care if it was fair. She smiled a witchy smile. "Besides, if I was a witch, a real witch, don't you think a lot of you would be toads, or broomsticks? or have warts on your noses? Big, horrible warts, the kind people can't stop staring at?"

When Mrs. Chemsky smiled like that, Mikey could almost believe the teacher could cast some horrible spells, picking out for each one of them something personally horrible. She almost positively liked Mrs. Chemsky, at that moment. She thought also that Margalo was positively brilliant.

"You're really bad," she murmured to Margalo, who was sitting there with her hair tucked behind her ear, looking harmless.

"Why thank you," Margalo said.

The soccer team practiced after school two days a week. At the first practice, the boys argued that girls didn't have cleats or shin guards and the coach pointed out that those could be purchased, so if those boys who were too upset to play, would they please stand aside, and let the rest of them . . . ? After some wind sprints followed by jogging around the field, after a series of passing and trapping drills, the coach divided them into teams for a scrimmage. He would run a couple of plays, then switch players around, from one team to another, from one position to another.

He settled Tanisha at wing, but Mikey wasn't fast enough for the forward line. Mikey argued that she could score, she was the kind of player who took goal shots, but the coach argued that if she couldn't keep up with her forwards, who cared how good her goal shots were. "How do I learn to run faster?" Mikey asked, but he couldn't help her with that, he said. "Try fullback," he said.

From his position as sweep, Louis Caselli thumbed his nose at her.

She kept coming up too far, crowding the halfbacks and the sweep, and then she had to run back when the ball got through; so the coach said, "You've really got energy, don't you? Why don't you try sweep, Mikey? You're aggressive enough."

"Aggressive is Mee-Shell's middle name," Louis Caselli said. "Oh, oops, I mean Porky. She doesn't like to be called Mee-Shell," he explained to the coach.

"You'd better sit out for fifteen minutes, Louis," the coach said.

Mikey thumbed her nose at Louis, and stuck her tongue out at him, and scored two goals just to show him what it was like when someone really good played the position.

As Louis ran back onto the field, he grabbed at her braid. She jabbed an elbow into his ribs. The coach tried putting Louis on Mikey's forward line, saying, "See if you can work together." Louis nodded, but when Mikey passed the ball forward to Tanisha rather than to him, for the sixth or sixteenth or twenty-sixth time, he lost it entirely. "You saw me, you stupid cow, I was free, I signaled, what do you think you're playing? Barbie? Pay attention, can't you at least pay attention to what's going on?"

"In a game, that kind of talk will get you a yellow card, Louis," the coach warned.

"Not for yelling at my own team," Louis objected.

"Louis."

"No, the goalies do it all the time. I've seen them on television."

"Lou-is."

"No, I have, they do. No ref ever cards a player for what he says to his own team."

"Why don't you get ready to go home, Louis," the coach said, calling him off the field. He advised Louis to settle down Right Now. That is, if Louis intended to be on the team?

Louis's mouth worked like a fish mouth for a minute, then he said, Yeah, he did want to play on the team.

The coach said Louis ought to want to, since they looked to be heading for a good season, and he turned back to the scrimmage, no longer interested in Louis.

The next morning, Mrs. Chemsky's fifth-grade class was still excited about the practice, and how right they had been to insist that both girls and boys be allowed to play on the school team. Tanisha greeted Mikey with the high sign. "We dusted 'em, sister. We had them dancing our music, didn't we even?"

"Didn't we even," Mikey agreed.

"You two talk as if you were the only ones on the team," Louis pointed out.

"Oh, were you there too, little man?" Tanisha asked, and she slapped her hand against her forehead. "Yo, Lou, gimme five."

So Louis did and "You, too, everybody," Mikey called, calling them in around, until about a quarter of the people in the class were at the front of the room, bumping hips and slapping hands.

Mrs. Chemsky gave this about one minute before she called them to order. She took attendance. "I hear good things about the soccer team," she announced.

"We're going to cream Riverside on Thursday," Louis said.

"Raise your hand when you have something to say, Louis," Mrs. Chemsky said. "Yes, Louis?"

"It's not just because of the girls," Louis said. "Even though that's what everyone's thinking. Soccer's a team sport."

"I think we all understand that," Mrs. Chemsky said. "Don't we, class?"

"Yes, Mrs. Chemsky," they all answered together.

* * *

The agreement, however, proved only a cease-fire, not a peace. The next morning, while heavy rain poured down outside, Louis Caselli turned into the devil incarnate.

Louis not only hid Hadrian Klenk's Red Sox cap, and denied it, and tripped Lee Cheung when Lee went up to sharpen pencils, and denied it, and trailed Henry Weisler, imitating his bouncy-toed walk, and denied that, too; he also kept up a steady quarrel with his cousins. Mrs. Chemsky could barely keep him quiet enough so the social studies class could continue.

At snack recess, while Mrs. Chemsky sat at her desk ignoring them, Rhonda explained the foulness of Louis's mood to anyone who cared to hear about it. "Louis is mad because Lynnie thinks he stinks. I mean, actually smells bad," she said. "You know, BO."

"Shut up, crybaby!" Louis yelled across the room. "Who told you that!"

"Told her what?" Margalo asked, all innocence.

"About me stinking," Louis sputtered. He broke a pencil in half.

"Nobody had to tell us," Mikey said. Louis threw both halves of the pencil at her, at the same time. So he missed her twice.

"Because he has a crush on Lynnie," Rhonda explained. "He's in looo-ve with Lynnie. Louis and

Lynnie, that's what he wants. Louis and Lynnie, sitting in a tree, k-i-s-s-i-n-g."

Lynnie ran out of the room.

"That's so stupid I do not, not for a minute!" Louis broke another pencil in half. This one he threw at Rhonda. She ducked, so he only hit her once. He kicked his desk and it flew into Justin's, and both desks crashed over.

People usually avoided Louis when he was in such a bad mood.

Not Mrs. Chemsky. She grabbed him by the shoulder, talked at him for a while out in the hallway, and left him sitting out there for twenty minutes, even though morning recess had ended. He missed the spelling pre-test and was going to have to go to Mr. Delaney's office during lunch recess to make it up where it would be quiet enough to concentrate.

It was Mikey he blamed, for everything.

But Mrs. Chemsky kept her eye on him so he couldn't do anything about all of the things he'd like to do to Mikey, except to hiss names at her the rest of the morning. "Mee-Shell." "Porky." "Blimpo."

His friends tried to get him cooled down. "We need her on the team. Shut up, man."

"Now," Margalo told Mikey the next morning, trading a snack Pop Tart for two oatmeal cookies with raisins that Mikey's mother had made just the day before, "Now, you have to quit."

Mikey was unwrapping the Pop Tart. "Strawberry. I love strawberry Pop Tarts." She bit into it, testing the sugary frosting and the sugary cakey pie crust and the sugary strawberry jam. "Quit what?"

"The team."

"What team?" The hand Mickey was feeding herself with stopped moving. "You don't mean the soccer team? But why would I do that?"

"Because then you can talk Tanisha and Rhonda into quitting, too."

"Why would I do that?"

"Because then you can start your own team, an all-girl one."

"Why would I want to do that?"

"Because," Margalo explained patiently, "then you can ask the coach to let you play the all-boy team, to see who gets to play for WSE in games. Against other schools. And keep Louis Caselli out, entirely."

Mikey got it. She smiled an evil coyote smile, her lips spread thin and her eyes narrowed. Then her smile faded. "What if we didn't win?"

Margalo had never thought of that. "I thought you were the best," she said.

"*I* am. But, there aren't enough girls to make a team, and the boys *are* pretty good."

"Oh," Margalo said.

"Was that always your plan? To start a girls' team?"

"I thought you wanted to get Louis."

Mikey thought for a minute, licking the last of the sugar off her fingers. "You're sort of sneaky, aren't you?"

Margalo had another suggestion. "What if you say you're thinking of quitting if Louis stays on the team. So he'd have to beg you to stay on it, which he'd do because he really wants to win. To be on the winning team. What if you and Tanisha just *say* you're thinking of starting a girls' team, but you don't have to mean it. You can tell Tanisha the plan if you want. But don't tell Rhonda," she said.

"You're *really* bad, aren't you?" Mikey said. She didn't think she could cook up that complicated a plan.

"Rhonda likes everyone to know she knows secrets," Margalo said. She was pretending not to hear what Mikey was saying, but she didn't pretend to herself. She was glad Mikey understood her. "That's why I told *her* about Louis and Lynnie," she boasted. "I don't mean to boast," she said then.

"*Really* devious," Mikey said, impressed. "How mean are you, inside?"

"Pretty mean," Margalo said. "But not to my friends. Not ever to my friends."

"Boy, I guess I better try to be your friend, then. Hadn't I?" Mikey laughed. Margalo looked so ordinary — ordinarily pretty, in her ordinary clothes, and with her round good-girl handwriting and her perfect spelling, the way she was well-behaved in class, her way of getting along with almost everybody. Nobody went after Margalo the way — for example — Louis Caselli went after Mikey, just for being who she was, just because he didn't like who she was.

Even Mikey liked Margalo.

Maybe there was something Margalo knew, if you wrote the same initials Me instead of ME.

Well, Mikey thought, she didn't feel like changing herself, even if she could.

Besides, knowing how mean Margalo was, inside — that made everything just fine. Mean inside was a quality Mikey could feel pretty friendly about. She was even getting curious about whether Margalo's meanness was about mischief more than anger.

Mikey knew that hers was more about anger than mischief.

She really wanted to smash Louis's face in. And hurt him. She didn't care about getting in trouble as long as she could get back at Louis Caselli.

"Look at the way he leads those boys around, they

all do what he tells them because they're afraid of him," she said to Margalo. "They're such wussies."

"He's only a bully," Margalo said.

"It's worse than that," Mikey insisted.

Margalo didn't argue. She was watching Lynnie return to the classroom, and go to stand behind Louis, where he and Sal and Justin and Harvey and David all stood around, looking at some old box Justin had, some airplane model kit it looked like. Nobody paid any attention to Lynnie until Louis turned around.

Margalo nudged Mikey, and pointed.

Lynnie was saying something.

Louis was denying it.

Lynnie was putting her hands on her hips and saying Ha-ha-ha, sarcastically.

Louis was denying it double, with red cheeks. He was looking around at his friends, who were looking back at him as if they thought he was probably lying.

Lynnie opened the top of the brown paper bag she was carrying. She turned it upside down and dumped papers — folded-up papers — notes — all over the floor.

Louis bent down and grabbed at them.

His friends tried to grab them, too, and faster.

Lynnie turned on her heel, and swept out, like a

queen. Her nose was up in the air as if she was the queen and Louis was some bug.

Some dirty black beetle bug that nobody would ever want to be in the same room with.

You'd go after him with Raid, or something, because you couldn't stand him, he made your skin creep.

Louis didn't even notice because he was grabbing at the papers his friends held. Harvey was opening one.

By now, almost the whole rest of the room was quiet, and Mrs. Chemsky had noticed.

By now, the noise level around Louis had roared up to a point where you couldn't miss it.

Margalo was smiling to herself. Mikey was enjoying it, but she suspected that Margalo knew more than she did, so she wasn't enjoying herself as much as she might have been, hearing Harvey read out "my heart thumps fast when you . . . ," watching Louis dive at Harvey, and knock him over, into Justin and David, and start punching at him.

Mrs. Chemsky was there in a second — in less than a second — she was there in a nanosecond.

Sal was trying to help Louis. He grabbed at the notes and stuffed them down the front of his shirt. But his shirt wasn't tucked in, so they dribbled right out again.

". . . right now you heard me," Mrs. Chemsky's voice took over the room.

Louis tried to jerk his arm free from her grasp, and — for just an instant — looked furious enough to forget that he was about to punch a teacher. And that the teacher was Mrs. Chemsky.

Margalo's hand was covering her mouth. Her eyes were so bright in her face, she looked as if someone was giving her a giant sundae, with three kinds of ice cream and three kinds of sauces, and whipped cream — fresh whipped cream, the real thing — piled so high on top it looked like a ship under sail.

"Oh," Margalo breathed.

Mikey could imagine how embarrassed and ashamed Louis must be feeling. She loved it.

Mrs. Chemsky hauled Louis off into the hall, "to regain control of himself," and the class was dead silent.

Listening.

The door stood open. They could hear Mrs. Chemsky, starting up, outside in the hallway. "Explain yourself, Louis Caselli," she was saying, her voice heavy with anger barely under control, one of the ways teachers had of letting you know that if they were your parents they would really be blowing their tops right now, really exploding at you, in whatever way your parents really exploded when you had done something really bad.

The door closed, before anyone could hear anything more from Louis than his heavy breathing.

After a silent while, Justin said, "Gees."

"What happened?" Ronnie asked. "Sal?"

Because she was his cousin, he had to answer her.

"Ask your friend Lynnie. She started it."

"Oh no, you can't blame me. I'm not the one who wrote those notes. Stupid notes, your stupid cousin, he's a pest. Yuck!" Lynnie turned to Ann for support, and Sharon joined in the murmurs of sympathy.

"I never liked him. Not a bit," Lynnie told Ann, and everyone else. "I would never in a hundred years."

"That's a lie," Sal said. "You said you'd go with him."

"Who says?"

"Louis told me. He asked you the first day of school. And you said. That was only two weeks ago in case you forgot. Liar."

"But I didn't *want* to," Lynnie protested.

"Then why did you say?"

She turned pink, turned away again, then turned back. "You can be sure I'm not going with him anymore. I bet nobody ever does, either, not even in high school."

Girls voiced their support of Lynnie's statement.

"Unless there's a girl who likes having a boy boast about having her for a girlfriend, even if she doesn't even read the stupid notes he writes to her, even if she tells him she doesn't want his stupid notes in her cubby," Lynnie said.

Girls shook their heads. The boys did, too, but more in amazement that one of their own could act like this than in agreement with whatever the girls were agreeing about.

Mikey whispered to Margalo. "Did he really boast? And how did she find out?"

Margalo just smiled.

Margalo looked so ordinary and nice.

"What if he finds out you're the one who started all this?" Mikey asked, a little worried because she didn't know if Margalo could fight back at Louis Caselli.

Margalo laughed, a nice ordinary laugh, and told Mikey, "He'll blame you."

Which is exactly what happened. When Louis returned to the classroom, he was hyper with righteous indignation. "It's none of his damn business. It's not fair — *not fair* — when he butts into my private life. Delaney called my parents!" he told his friends.

"Yeah," they said, "we know. Yeah. Yeah. It's tough, man."

"Someone must've told," Louis said.

"Yeah. Bad 'cess, man."

"Settle down now, Louis. Class," Mrs. Chemsky warned. "Quiet."

"And I can guess who," Louis said.

He gave Mikey the bad eye — she told Margalo, Louis didn't know how to do an evil eye, the worst he could get was a bad eye; which made Margalo laugh, which wasn't a good idea when Louis was already het up. Whenever he had a chance to turn his head in his front row seat and pretend he was looking at someone else, he gave Mikey the bad eye. When he didn't have a chance to turn around, she could feel the heat of his glaring because it bounced off the chalkboard at her, like some reflected laser beam.

Louis Caselli was really angry.

It was almost exciting, Mikey thought. She wasn't going to let him scare her. She wasn't about to rat on Margalo, either.

This was war. So it was a battle move when she refused to play in the lunchtime soccer game. It was a hint about more refusals to come.

"Chicken," Louis called. "But not Chicken Little. Chicken Big. She knows I'll get her and she's scared. Heap Big Chicken."

"Is that what you think?" Mikey called back.

Louis's eyes were practically whirling in his head like whirligigs, he was so angry.

Mikey felt like giggling. "Maybe I don't feel like playing soccer. Maybe, I've outgrown it."

If his eyes could have bugged out any more, or spun any faster, Louis Caselli's eyes would have popped out of their sockets.

Mikey laughed out loud.

Louis grabbed at her braid.

She punched him in the throat.

He stumbled back a step, then recovered to punch her in the stomach.

"Ooomph."

"You didn't think I'd dare hit you!" Louis crowed, until her fist landed next to his left eye and then he complained, "You're just trying to make me look dumb."

"You do that," she panted, "all by yourself." Excited, and afraid, her heart beat so fast she couldn't catch her breath. She didn't know what he would do next. "You don't need my help." And she punched him in the nose.

Once again, Louis Caselli's nose started to ooze blood.

Mikey didn't know if she'd gone too far, but she didn't know what else to do except continue.

"Mikey? just ignore him," she heard Margalo call.

"He's just mad because he knows the team hasn't got a chance unless you're on it. Because Tanisha won't stay on either, will you, Tanisha? Because Mikey was thinking of trying to have an all-girl team for WSE. Maybe an all-girl team could play for WSE. That would be cool, don't you think?"

"Would be different," Tanisha answered, grinning.

"But what about us?" the boys asked.

"Would you really want to play on a just-girls team?" Rhonda asked. "I wouldn't."

"But Mikey," Justin said. "That's not fair. First you make us let you play, and then you quit. You aren't going to do that, are you?"

Mikey smiled at Louis, a brand-new, level-four mean smile she had never even thought of before. "Depends," she said.

She let them all think out what it might depend on, like, maybe she wouldn't want to play on any team Louis Caselli was playing on.

She let Louis see that if the team had to choose between being a team with Louis Caselli on it, or a team with Mikey Elsinger on it, most of them would choose her.

Louis was standing there watching, blood running over the finger he held up against his nostrils. His face got pale and he blinked — a couple of hard blinks. "I got to get some ice," he said.

Nobody followed him off the playground.

Mikey geared down to a level-two mean smile. "So, anyone want to play soccer?" she asked.

Of course they did.

It was a complete victory for Mikey. Margalo should get the credit, as Mikey knew, but everyone — including Louis — knew it was a complete Mikey victory.

So she shouldn't have been surprised when Louis did something crazy, that afternoon. Anyway, she guessed she shouldn't have been. Afterwards. But afterwards, even Margalo admitted that even she never thought anything like that would happen.

What happened was: Louis took a pair of big scissors and took advantage of the way in art class people wandered all around the room, if they wanted, to look at other people's work, and he came up behind Mikey and lifted her braid up and cut it off.

It wasn't that easy, but he had big sharp scissors, and he did it so quietly, it was finished before anybody noticed that he was doing something really weird. Mikey barely got her hand up, to feel what was going on before he'd amputated her long braid.

Then he crowed like an Indian, and did a crowing Indian victory war dance, *Whoop! Whoop!* He was waving the braid above his head, like a scalp in a movie.

The braid was a foot and a half long. It started to come unraveled, as he waved it around.

Everybody got quiet. And scared.

Mrs. Chemsky stayed in the room during art, working at her desk. Mrs. Scott leaned over Mikey's desk, as if she wanted to hide what had happened from Mrs. Chemsky.

Mikey stood up, and stared right at the thing in Louis's hand, and she looked right into Louis's blue eyes. The thing looked like some dead weasel, or something. Louis looked like he was already sorry.

Well, he'd be a lot sorrier.

"That was really stupid, Louis," Mikey said to him.

"Even for you," she added.

Slowly, she walked out of the room. She didn't ask to be excused, or anything. Mrs. Chemsky didn't try to stop her, and neither did Mrs. Scott, who was asking her daughter What was going on here. It was possible for Mikey to get into the girls' bathroom unimpeded, and get herself closed into one of the cubicles. She sat down on the toilet, but she hadn't pulled down her jeans.

Her right hand felt the back of her head. She was probably in shock, she thought. She was probably in traumatic shock.

She saw Margalo's sneakers, and the blue socks Margalo was wearing, folded down into a cuff. Margalo was standing right on the other side of the cubicle door.

Mikey wished Margalo would go away.

Mikey was really glad she was there.

"I know you're crying," Margalo said.

"No, I'm not," Mikey said. But her stuffy nose gave it away: She wanted to cry and she might be about to.

"I don't mind," Margalo said. "I'm going to stay here."

"None of my business what you do," Mikey said.

She sat on the toilet and cried as quietly as she could for as short as she could. Then she practiced taking deep breaths, deep breath in, deep breath out, deep breath in, until she could tell Margalo, "My mother is going to have kittens. She's been growing my hair since first grade." She blew her nose into some toilet paper.

Margalo sympathized. "I'm sorry, Mikey."

"You didn't cut my braid off."

"But it's my fault. I mean —"

"I'm looking on the bright side," Mikey said. Now she felt like standing up, and dropping the toilet paper into the bowl, and flushing, and coming out into the bathroom. "I never wanted long hair. It's a pain to take care of."

"I mean, about Louis," Margalo said. And then — looking right at Mikey — she started laughing. As soon as she started up laughing, a few little tears came out of her eyes. She wiped them away with her hand. "And I'm sorry because you weren't supposed to get hurt. It's *your* hair that's gone, and I didn't ever think — but he's in real trouble now. Louis is. We really did drive him crazy. I mean, this was really crazy and we did it."

Mikey tried to laugh, too, but she couldn't. So she tried on a smile, a Celebration smile for the downfall of Louis Caselli, but all she could do was cry. Not much, just kind of leaky faucet crying, and it wasn't loud, but. . . .

"I had no idea," Margalo said. "Did you? Have any idea?"

Mikey shook her head.

And it seemed to her that maybe some of the feelings she was having, that were coming out as tears, were just surprise. "Attacked from the rear," she said. "Shot from behind, shot in the back. Ambushed, bushwhacked — d'you think we got him expelled?" Mikey asked, then, and then she was smiling a real Celebration smile, a *We-won-the-war* smile. Because a lot of her feelings were just plain excitement. She had no idea what was going to happen next, but something.

"You look pretty terrible," Margalo said.

Mikey moved over to the mirror. Her face was

blotched red and white, her eyes were swollen and pink. "Yeah," she agreed.

"Everybody is going to feel so sorry for you —"

"I'm always ugly when I cry. I look like a pound of hamburger."

"You'll be the most popular girl in the class. Anyway, for the afternoon."

"I'm not going in there looking like this."

"You want to go home?"

Mikey shook her head. She turned on the cold water and started splashing at her face, to cool it down. She took one of the paper towels and soaked it in cold water, and held it over her eyes, to reduce the swelling. "Get me some ice, will you?"

"I can't," Margalo said. "Where would I?"

"From the teachers' lounge. Don't they have a refrigerator?"

"You look sort of tragic," Margalo said.

"I look sort of dumb, and like I've been crying," Mikey said. "Like I'm a Rhonda Ransom clone."

Margalo didn't say anything. Mikey peeled away the wet paper towel and looked at Margalo, hard. "What?"

"Nothing," Margalo said. "I'm thinking."

"How to get me a new face?"

"Quiet," Margalo said. "Let me think," she said, but then she went on right away, "I'll be right back.

You wait here. Bathe your eyes," she said, like she was some beautician.

Mikey gave her a snarly smile.

"You'll see," Margalo said. She let the bathroom door swing behind her, and ran down the hall back to the classroom.

Miss Carter, the school secretary, was at Mrs. Chemsky's desk. She stared at Margalo. So did everybody else in the class, which didn't include Louis Caselli. Miss Carter put a finger to her lips. Margalo approached the teacher's desk and whispered the request to get Mikey's jacket. "She's upset," Margalo whispered.

"Of course," Miss Carter whispered back.

Margalo took down her own jacket, because Mikey's was a windbreaker that had an elastic hem. Her own jacket was longer, and didn't have an elastic bottom. Hers zipped up to the neck and then on up to the pointed tips of the collar, which was what she was looking for, a jacket that zipped up high.

In the bathroom, Mikey still had a soggy brown towel over her eyes, but when Margalo had explained the plan, she balled it up in her hand and tossed it into the trash. "We should wait, to be sure Mrs. Chemsky is back," Mikey said.

"You can get ready," and Margalo unbuttoned the button-down stepbrother shirt she was wearing.

Mikey took off her long-sleeved T-shirt. They exchanged shirts, and then Margalo pulled the neck of her stepbrother's shirt up over Mikey's head, and did up the top button so it wouldn't slip down. She reached in the neck and pulled out some of Mikey's thick, now chin-length hair.

Mikey peeped out between buttons to see herself in the mirror. She was starting to enjoy herself.

Margalo helped her into the jacket, pulled the collar up over her head, zipped it, and pulled the hair out again.

"I can't see a thing," Mikey complained.

"I'll hold onto your arm, like this. I'll warn you about steps, or doors, or anything."

"You promise?"

"Promise."

"Will you keep your promise?"

"Of course. Otherwise, what's the point?"

Mikey subsided. "And it smells, too. You need to wash your jacket," she said.

"Are you ready?" Margalo asked. She knew her jacket needed washing. She didn't need Mikey telling her that. Mikey was an only child who got to do her own laundry. Margalo took hold of Mikey's left arm with her right hand. She held Mikey behind the elbow, like she'd seen people do for blind people on TV.

"Promise you'll keep your promise," Mikey said

again. The layers of clothing she was buttoned and zipped into muffled her voice.

"I promise," Margalo said, exasperated.

"Because I can't see, so I have to trust you. Not to run me into walls or something."

Margalo hadn't even thought of that. She was sorry, now, she'd given her word. She wondered if she really *had* to keep her promise.

She knew she did, but for a few seconds she wondered.

They went down the hall, Mikey looking like some space alien, with hundreds of skinny antennae instead of a head, probably with miniature eyes at the end of the feelers. Mikey looked like her face had gotten lost, or left behind somewhere. Their entrance interrupted Mrs. Chemsky's speech. "Come in, girls," Mrs. Chemsky said. "Sit down."

Everybody stared, while Margalo guided Mikey to her seat. When Margalo wanted to say something, like "look out here," she spoke very softly to the turned-up collar. When Mikey asked, "Aren't we back yet?" Margalo leaned toward the zipped neck to listen, because between the muffling and the low voice, nobody could hear whatever it was that Mikey said.

She helped Mikey sit, and then went to her own desk.

Mrs. Chemsky looked at Mikey, whose hair was

sticking up out of the neck of the jacket. She looked at Margalo, who widened her eyes innocently.

"I'm sure we are all very sorry," Mrs. Chemsky said to Mikey. "You have all of our sympathy, Miss Elsinger."

Mikey muttered something.

Margalo leaned over to hear what it was.

Then Margalo leaned back. "She says," Margalo said, "she knows."

The class was entirely quiet.

"I want to ask you to take off the jacket, Miss Elsinger," Mrs. Chemsky said.

The jacket turned in its seat, towards Margalo.

"Miss Elsinger?"

The jacket turned back to face Mrs. Chemsky.

"Will you please take off your jacket?"

The jacket leaned towards Margalo. Who listened. Everyone could see she was listening.

"Does she have to?"

"Yes," Mrs. Chemsky said, firmly, "she has to."

The jacket turned towards Margalo.

"She doesn't want to," Margalo said.

"We understand that," Mrs. Chemsky said, sympathetically. "That's all I'll ask of you for the rest of the afternoon, Miss Elsinger," she said sympathetically.

The jacket turned towards Margalo. It nodded its collar, up and down, Yes.

Everybody watched. If Mikey had been dying of poison, she wouldn't have had more of everyone's attention.

Margalo reached out and held onto the two points of the collar, holding them up so she could pull the zipper down. She unzipped the jacket completely. Then she let its two halves separate and helped Mikey take it off.

A shirt, with a burst of thick brown hair coming out of its buttoned neck, sat in Mikey's seat. The shirt faced Mrs. Chemsky, even though it couldn't see her.

Mrs. Chemsky stared at the shirt.

Margalo bit at the inside of her mouth, to keep from laughing.

She could bet Mikey was grinning away, invisible under the shirt.

Mrs. Chemsky stared at Margalo.

Margalo put a wide-eyed, worried, sympathetic expression on her face, and busily tucked her hair behind both of her ears with both of her hands.

Rhonda Ransom spoke. "That's not fair."

"Did you raise your hand, Rhonda?" Mrs. Chemsky asked. "Yes, Rhonda?"

"It's not — they changed shirts. They wanted to trick you," Rhonda said. "Are you going to let them get away with it?"

"I think we've had all the excitement I can take

for one afternoon," Mrs. Chemsky said. "So let's get back to work. Perhaps, Margalo," she said, "you will take out Miss Elsinger's social studies book for her, and open it to page thirty-six. And your own, too, of course, since you are being so very helpful."

"Yes, Mrs. Chemsky," Margalo said, all cooperation and obedience.

4

Getting Louis Caselli Back

Louis Caselli was suspended from school for four days. Moreover, when he returned they would switch him into Ms Spalding's fifth grade. Mrs. Chemsky reported this to her thirty students.

Her mother kept Mikey home from school for a day, to take her into the city and have her hair fixed. Everyone was amazed at how Mikey looked, how good she looked, and said so, over and over. The day after that, she came to school with green hair.

"It's like broccoli," Margalo greeted her.

"It shampoos out. Gradually. The box said."

"Like broccoli somebody sat on," Margalo said.

"I think I'll try purple, next," Mikey said. "Or maybe a henna rinse. Do you think I'd look good with red hair?"

"Why not blonde?"

"Blonde is too ordinary," Mikey said. "Look at Rhonda."

"I do not!" Rhonda denied it. "My mother wouldn't let me even *think* of it. I don't know what kind of mother you have that lets you dye *your* hair."

All the girls looked closely at Rhonda's shining hair.

"Or maybe I'll just have it frosted," Mikey said. "Tipped with gold." She ran her fingers through her thick, short, green hair.

"Great," Margalo approved, sarcastically. "Great idea, Mikey. Great style touch."

"I'll do yours for you, if you want," Mikey offered.

They had an audience of almost everyone in the class. They were like a comedy routine team, like Bert and Ernie, like Murphy Brown and Corky. They were onstage, stage center, and they both loved it.

"But what about my cousin?" Salvatore Caselli asked, then. Something not fair was going on, he knew it. He just couldn't put his finger on exactly what it was. Louis shouldn't have cut off the braid, Sal knew that, but Louis couldn't help it: He'd lost his temper.

Louis had gotten into the worst trouble he'd ever been in, in a long school career of getting into trouble. And Mikey didn't even care about her hair.

She didn't even care, *and* she dyed it green. None of the Casellis had ever dared dye his hair green. Or her hair, except the Caselli girls would never want to.

"My cousin's been thrown out of our class," Sal reminded everyone.

"He deserved it," was the general opinion. Margalo and Mikey didn't say anything, and that made Louis look even worse. "Look what he did to Mikey."

"He didn't dye her hair green. He just cut it."

"But Sal, he shouldn't have. You know that," Ronnie reminded him. "*You* know that, whatever anyone at home says."

Ronnie had reported to Margalo, *Lotsa flak at home, everybody blaming someone else besides Louis, and yelling, they really think Mikey was asking for it.* "*That girl must have done something to make our Louis so angry.*"

"She made him do it," Sal argued now.

"Oh, right," everyone agreed. "That's right, she put the scissors in his hand and put a gun to his head and ordered him to cut. Or else."

"No, but it's true," Sal protested. "It's not *fair.*"

Margalo and Mikey knew he was right, but they didn't care. They pushed their desks together at lunch, as usual. The whole class was on their side, except Sal, and it was OK for Sal to be loyal to his cousin. "How about peanut butter?" Mikey asked, with a self-satisfied smirk of a smile, which had nothing to do with peanut butter. "I hate it."

"Me, too, and the worst is peanut butter and jelly sandwiches —"

"Yeah." Mikey smirked away, thinking about peanut butter and Louis Caselli.

"No, the worst is those peanut butter and cheese cracker packages my mother buys by the carton, to put into the little kids' lunches. Not mine. She knows better than to try to feed me those things. Although," Margalo said, pulling the top slice of supermarket white bread up to be sure there was mustard on her bologna sandwich, "I do like peanut butter cups."

"Anything with chocolate is good," Mikey agreed. She had a cheese, tomato, and sprout sandwich, on multigrain bread, with mayonnaise. "Want to trade halves?"

They traded.

Margalo looked down at the two sandwich halves on her desk. "Like yin and yang," she said.

"Who are they?"

"It's Oriental," Margalo said.

"We could ask Lee about them," Mikey suggested. She suspected Margalo of having a crush on Lee Cheung, who decorated the borders on all of his papers, and already in only the first weeks of school had succeeded in irritating Mrs. Chemsky, because he wouldn't stop doing that. Mrs. Chemsky had strict rules about how papers should look when they were handed in. No Decorated Margins was one of them. Mikey watched Margalo's face carefully, when she mentioned Lee's name. "He'd know."

"*You* can ask Lee if you want to, but not while I'm around, please." Margalo knew what Mikey suspected and she made a point of feeding those suspicions. She knew who she really had a crush on and it wasn't Lee Cheung. But she didn't feel like telling anyone who, not even a friend. If they were friends. Mikey felt like a friend.

"Yin and yang is those two fish, inside the same circle," Margalo said. "One is black and the other is white, and their eye — each one's eyes, that is —"

"I know what you mean," Mikey said, remembering jewelry stores. "It's the color of the other fish."

Margalo was nodding her head. "Opposites are — where opposites run into each other is where things happen." Margalo was thinking what a relief it was not to be talking about TV shows or clothing or bands, what fun it was to tell someone what your real ideas were. "Like us," Margalo said. "When we get together things happen."

"Except," Mikey pointed out, offering Margalo half an orange, for which Margalo exchanged half a plastic container of chocolate pudding, and half of the banana for dipping into it. Margalo had her eye on the two big squares of linzer torte in Mikey's lunch box.

"Except, we're the same, not opposite," Mikey said. That was pretty interesting. They were pretty interesting, she and Margalo. She had to admit, she hoped they were getting to be friends.

That thought made her so nervous she almost smiled a level-two mean smile at Margalo, just to be safe. But she didn't because Margalo said then, "I told my mother about you. I told her how we're almost exactly alike."

Mikey couldn't *imagine* Margalo's mother. "I bet she was thrilled."

"She said 'That's nice, dear.' Well, the baby was throwing up," Margalo said. "On her lap, and she was wearing a rayon skirt, that has to be dry-cleaned," Margalo said.

"I did, too," Mikey admitted, offering a square of linzer torte, the raspberry jam oozing dark red between golden-brown lattices. "You want this?"

"Yes. Please." Margalo bit into it, and felt the flavor fill her mouth. "Good, it's so — *you* threw up into your mother's lap?"

Mikey laughed. "No, I told her about you. She's been on my case. '*Are you making any friends, yet? Are you trying hard enough? Do you have a little friend you'd like to ask over?'* That kind of thing. I told her," Mikey added, with one of her sarcastic *I-ask-you* smiles, "that I didn't think *little* described anybody I was likely to be friends with, at my age."

"What did she say? About me," Margalo asked.

"Oh, she wanted details — how tall, what shade of brown hair, family, what your father does, does your mother work, do you have brothers and sisters, where do you live, you know the kind of questions. She doesn't think we're all that much alike. Although she did say that us both being born in Rochester was an odd coincidence."

"Do you agree with her?"

"Well, I mean, you're tall and thin, and I'm not, and your hair is straight —"

"And thin."

"—and mine's thick, I mean, I'm sort of round and thick and you're sort of straight and thin, so we don't look alike at all."

"Not to mention that my hair isn't green. Maybe I will dye it green."

"But my mother always tries to get me to agree with her."

"Well, at least she pays attention to you when you talk."

"Well, I wish she wouldn't."

"Well, I wish mine would. Sometimes. Like I'm a real person, by myself, a real person, not just a job."

"So she can catch my mistakes and tell me what's righter."

"As if I was interesting. Me. Me myself by myself."

"Me, too."

"Me, too, exactly," Margalo sighed. "*Will* you tell me how to dye my hair?"

"Green?"

"Or purple? If you can do it, so can I. And it washes out, and hair grows anyway, so whatever happens to hair is only temporary. Like you said."

"You don't think your mother would notice," Mikey guessed.

"She'd probably *notice*," Margalo said. She was packing up her trash, the paper towel and snack-pack container and banana peel, the Saran Wrap from around her sandwich; the plastic spoon she returned to her lunch box to be washed, and reused. "I just don't think she'd have the time, or the energy, to care. So it would be fine. And my brothers would be jealous."

"Not your sisters?"

Margalo shook her head.

"You always know how people will react," Mikey said.

"No, I don't. Do I? Well, maybe I do. Don't you?"

"If I did, I wouldn't have noticed that you do."

"You don't have to get angry."

"I'm not."

"You sound it."

"That's not angry."

"Oh yeah? Then what is it?"

"It's — I don't know. It's the voice inside my head. That's what I sound like inside my head."

"Oh," Margalo said. She sat and thought for a minute. "Then you must be pretty angry. Inside."

"Only when I don't like what's going on."

"Oh," Margalo said, and thought for a minute. Then she said, "You don't often like what's going on, do you? I mean, you know what I mean, don't get angry, or, don't get angry at me, but I want to ask you about something else anyway. I want to ask you, what about Louis?"

"Louis good-riddance-to-bad-rubbish Caselli? What about him?" At the reminder of Louis, Mikey felt like she might be smiling some kind of Cheerios happy-face smile. And that felt weird.

"Do you want to try and get Louis back into the class?" Margalo asked.

"Why would I want to do *that*?"

"To see if we can."

"But, Margalo," Mikey protested, "if we did that, he'd be back in the class."

"I know, but —"

"I thought you wanted to get him, as much as I did."

"I do, but — I did, but I bet we *could* do it, get him thrown out, first, and then get him allowed back. He wouldn't dare be the same as he was before."

Mikey doubted that.

"Watch at recess," Margalo predicted confidently.

"He's not allowed out for recess," Mikey reminded her. And smiled: *Victory.*

At recess, Rhonda didn't play soccer. She was wearing a new outfit, she explained, and she had forgotten to bring shorts to change into, also she didn't have her sneakers. She held out her foot to show them her new black leather skimmers. She hadn't had time that morning, and she slept late, she explained. And anyway, she had really been looking for a chance to ask "all of you," she said, looking around —

Her eyes failed to focus on Margalo. Rhonda didn't even *see* Margalo standing there with Doucelle and Derrie.

"What I *really* want to ask," Rhonda said, "is about how unfair it is for Louis to have to get put into the other class. Don't you think?"

They looked at one another until Ronnie said, "Well, he's my cousin, and I don't mind him. But —"

"She *wanted* to get him in trouble," Rhonda interrupted. "She did it on purpose."

Margalo stayed quiet. She knew that if she stayed quiet, Rhonda would assume she didn't *dare* speak. Rhonda Ransom only saw things being the way she wanted. She was the kind of person who wants to be queen so she can chop off peoples' heads, but she also wants everyone to like her, which means pretending to be nice. In his favor, Margalo had to admit, Louis never pretended that.

"And that isn't fair. Is it?" Rhonda insisted.

"The teachers decided what was fair," Ann said. "What can we do, anyway?"

"Well I for one am never going to speak to Mee-Shell again, that's one thing I can do," Rhonda announced. "As far as I'm concerned, she is *in*-visible. I think that's a pretty good idea. If we all do that. . . ."

"Louis *did* cut off her braid. That braid was more than halfway down her back," Derrie said, developing her case like a TV lawyer, "which means that her hair might have been as long as practically to her waist. It takes a long time to grow hair that long, and he just cut it off."

"She doesn't care," Rhonda announced.

Derrie ignored Rhonda. "As if it's all right to just — destroy something of somebody else's. It's the same as if he ripped up a report she'd written. That's never all right."

"She dyed her hair green," Rhonda pointed out. "How much can she care?"

"It's not about Mikey," Doucelle said. "It's about how Louis shouldn't have cut her hair."

"She kept hitting him."

"He hit her back," Ann said. "The teachers think this is fair."

"She started it," Rhonda maintained.

"He called her names," Doucelle reminded them.

"She shouldn't act like she's so tough if she can't take people being mean back."

"Neither should he," was Derrie's opinion.

"Well, I just don't think it was fair to Louis. He's been in our class since first grade."

"Since kindergarten," Ronnie said. "Actually. You just didn't come until first grade, Rhonda," she said.

"Well anyway, I think we ought to be loyal to Louis. And do something."

"What?"

"Well. *I'm* going to ask Mrs. Chemsky if he can come back into our class. I'm going to ask in front of everyone, too, so that Mee-Shell will know that everyone knows she wanted to get him in trouble. And nobody wants to talk to her. Like me."

None of the girls said anything. "See?" Rhonda said, then went over to where Lindsey and Sharon and Karen had been waiting for her. She showed them her new shoes.

Doucelle drew lines for four-square in the dirt. "I wish the school had a volleyball net. Volleyball's fun, and an Olympic sport, too," she said, dragging her sneaker in the dirt.

Margalo could say something about that. "Can't we just play something? Does it have to be an Olympic sport? Can't we just play for *fun*?"

Doucelle admitted, "Truth is, I don't like soccer. Volleyball's a team sport, too," she said.

"So's football," Ronnie argued.

"Football's what boys think a team sport is," Derrie said.

They all laughed about that, but "I'm right," she said.

"So do we ask Mrs. Chemsky? For a volleyball net, and a couple of volleyballs," Doucelle stuck to her point. "And volleyball's a game boys and girls play on the same team. Annaliese, would you or Ronnie ask her? You're old students."

"You've been here almost three weeks," Annaliese answered. "You'd have a better chance, too, because you're African-American, so you're the one who should. And your mother's another teacher, you've got the best chance of any of us. But what do you think about Louis? Rhonda will ask for him back, you can bet on it."

Margalo thought she had good advice, and she gave it. "If you wait to ask about volleyball until after Rhonda — I bet Mrs. Chemsky says no to Rhonda, and after a teacher has said no to something, if something else comes along and she can say yes to it, she likes to."

"Do you really think she'll say no to Rhonda?" Ronnie asked. "Do you think she ought to? Mikey's your friend, what do you think?"

"I think," Margalo answered carefully, "that I feel sort of sorry for Louis Caselli. He's had it his own way for so long. . . . He didn't know what he was getting into with Mikey. He thought, he could just run things the way he wants to. He just didn't know, you know? What he was up against."

They liked that idea. "You mean, Mikey?"

"I mean her, and me, too, and all of us. Fifth-grade girls. He thought, we were still little girls he could push around, and we'd be afraid of him, that's what I think. Even though I'm new, I think that's what he must have been like. Now he can't have his own way anymore. Don't *you* feel sort of sorry for him?"

At the start of math, Rhonda raised her hand.

"Yes, Rhonda?"

"Mrs. Chemsky?"

"Yes, Rhonda."

"I was wondering. That is, a lot of us are wondering, everyone wonders —"

There was a pause.

"Wonders what, Rhonda?"

"About Louis?"

"What about Louis?"

"If he can come back into this class? Because we don't think it's fair. We don't think it's at all fair. Because it wasn't just *his* fault, you know."

"I think everyone knows that it takes two to tango," Mrs. Chemsky said.

"Yes," Rhonda agreed. "I see what you mean," Rhonda said. "What's tango?" Rhonda asked.

"A dance, Argentine in origin, I believe. The tango is a ballroom dance that became popular during the twenties, Rhonda."

"Oh, well, I see now. We don't do that dance anymore, Mrs. Chemsky."

"I'm aware of that, Rhonda," Mrs. Chemsky said. And waited again.

"So will you?"

"Will I what, Rhonda?"

"Let Louis back into our class."

"It's not up to me," Mrs. Chemsky said.

"It isn't?"

"No, Rhonda. Class, take out your homework papers, please. Yes, Rhonda?"

"Does that mean you won't? Let Louis back in?"

"No, Rhonda, it doesn't. It means that the final decision doesn't rest with me, and it means also that you haven't given me any compelling reason to think I ought to reopen the question with Mr. Delaney and the rest of the faculty."

"But I told you, everybody wants it."

"Yes, but everybody *always* wants something," Mrs. Chemsky said. "That is the normal human condition and therefore doesn't constitute a compelling reason. Moreover, I don't imagine that everybody in this class does want Louis back. Take your math paper and textbook out now, Rhonda. We are waiting for you."

Rhonda did as she was told, muttering to herself, mumbling.

"I bet we could," Margalo whispered to Mikey. "Wanna try?"

"You must be kidding."

"Girls," Mrs. Chemsky warned them.

"To show we *can* do it," Margalo whispered. Then she smiled right at Mrs. Chemsky, and drew her fingers across her lips as if she was zipping them closed.

Mrs. Chemsky didn't smile back.

"To show everyone who's really in charge," Margalo muttered, out of the side of her mouth.

Mikey snorted, and tried to pretend she was coughing.

"That's two, Miss Elsinger," Mrs. Chemsky said. "Three strikes and you're out," she warned, to be sure that Mikey — and especially everyone else watching Mikey — knew whose classroom this was. "Yes, Doucelle?"

"Before we start, I want to ask. Could you ask Mr. Delaney to get us a volleyball net, and a ball, so we could play volleyball at recess?" Doucelle said.

Mrs. Chemsky hesitated, thinking that over, and answered, "I would be happy to talk about that with you, at the end of the day, Doucelle. It's a very good idea, but math period isn't the best time to discuss how I can help you with it."

At morning recess the next day, Margalo wanted to plan out what Mikey should do, and say, and how to organize the rest of the girls — and any of the boys, too, like Noah, who was smart enough to see sense, and Ira, who wasn't afraid of either Louis or Mikey, and maybe Hadrian Klenk, too, even though he was pretty chicken, because he had a mind of his own. Not counting Louis Caselli's pack of followers among the people she asked for support was one of Margalo's favorite parts of her plan.

But Mikey didn't even want to talk about it.

"Why not? I thought we —" Margalo argued.

Mikey didn't want to listen. "It's *my* hair. *I'm* the one he hates."

"You're the one who hates him, too."

"I just want to beat him," Mikey said. "I just want him to know how much better I am than he is."

"Why don't you want me to help out?" Margalo asked.

"Because," Mikey said. "Just because. Because I want to do it myself. Because I'm the one he was picking on."

"Even if that was your own fault? and you picked the fights, too?"

Mikey just smiled. She didn't say anything. Neither did Margalo.

Like Rhonda, Mikey waited until just before math class to raise her hand.

"Yes, Miss Elsinger?" Mrs. Chemsky asked.

"It's about Louis," Mikey said.

"What about Louis?" Mrs. Chemsky's voice was wary. She stood very still, at the front of the classroom. Everybody else had been surprised, also, and they were all listening closely. Mrs. Chemsky looked from Margalo, who looked right back at her, to Mikey.

"I think he ought to come back into our class," Mikey said.

"That's *my* idea," Rhonda objected.

The people around her desk shushed her.

"So can he?" Mikey asked.

Lame, she sounded really lame. She should have let Margalo help her think about what to say. She knew that now. She hadn't planned out what she would say; she had only planned when she would raise her hand to ask.

"But it was," Rhonda muttered. "I thought of it first. Yesterday. She's stealing my idea."

Denise turned to whisper, "Can't you let it go? Just for a minute?"

"I must admit, Miss Elsinger, you surprise me," Mrs. Chemsky said. "You're the last person I expected to hear from."

"I guess," Mikey agreed.

"May I ask what changed your mind?" Mrs. Chemsky asked.

"I didn't change my mind," Mikey told her. Now that there was something to quarrel with she had more to say, and words came more easily. "I just think — it's fairer if he's in the class."

"That's what *I* said, yesterday," Rhonda complained. "You all heard me."

Mikey remembered, then, something Margalo had pointed out. "It's *my* hair," she said, "that he cut off. Hair grows, so mine will grow back. Not that what he did wasn't bad," she said. "But — it would be better if he were back in our class, because — he's in our class," she concluded lamely.

Mrs. Chemsky looked at her for a minute, as if trying to see past the bones to the inside of her head. The whole class waited. Silent. Not daring to move, because that might jiggle the teacher. They could tell she was thinking about how it might be done. Getting Louis back. *No jiggling,* you could almost hear the unspoken warning going around the classroom.

"Well," Mrs. Chemsky finally said.

They all waited.

"I could talk with Mr. Delaney," Mrs. Chemsky said.

They all breathed out. Mikey turned to grin at Margalo, a grin like a punch in the nose.

"If that *is* what we want to do. Now, class," Mrs. Chemsky said, before they could start getting excited, "we've heard that some people feel it isn't fair to remove Louis from our classroom and we have heard that the person against whom he committed his offense is willing to forgive him. I know —" she added, before Mikey could say anything. "That isn't exactly what you said, Miss Elsinger. Grant me the simplification. I want to ask the class — I would like to ask for a vote on this question, before I take it to Mr. Delaney. Unless we're agreed, there's no sense in troubling him, or Louis. It will also be practice for when we elect class officers, which we'll be doing soon. First things first, however. A vote is meant to be preceded by open discussion. Is there any further argument anyone would like to present, either for or against? Yes, Rhonda?"

"It's not fair on Louis," she said. "Just like I said, yesterday. It's what I already said."

"Thank you, Rhonda. Does anyone — yes, Joshua?"

"Like, it's our class," Joshua said. "So we should, like, get to say, if someone is — like — thrown out."

"You really think it's our class?" Harvey Smith said. "Man, if that's what you really think, you are seriously ignorant."

"Yes, Hadrian?" Mrs. Chemsky said, ignoring Harvey.

"It *is* our class, because if we want to we can entirely disrupt it. It's really up to us, whether the teacher can teach or not," Hadrian said.

"Does that have anything to do with Louis?" Mrs. Chemsky inquired.

"I was talking about getting to vote about Louis," Hadrian said. "Because a class is sort of a democracy. Except, it's not representative. But we're all responsible. Isn't that right?"

"If I understand you, yes, I would agree," Mrs. Chemsky said, carefully. "However, I'm not sure I do understand you, Hadrian. But that is beside the point. Does anyone else —? Yes, Lindsey?"

"What if he does it again?"

"That," Mikey announced, "will be someone else's problem. I'm out of hair, myself."

If a vote had been taken right then for the list of popular people, Mikey would have been on it.

"Yes, Lindsey?"

"I wasn't making a joke. Louis is — he has a bad temper, and he distracts the class, and he's bossy. It's easier to learn in class without Louis. I don't care if you tell him I said that, Sal, because it's true and we all know it."

It *was* true. They all *did* know it. Suddenly, the question wasn't so simple. Suddenly, it wasn't going to be so easy to vote.

"Yes, Margalo?"

"I think it's better if there are two people in the class who boss other people around, because they cancel each other out and there's not just one Hitler running things."

"I don't know that anyone in this class can qualify as a Hitler, Margalo," Mrs. Chemsky said. "Now, are we ready to vote?"

"What did you mean by that?" Mikey hissed at Margalo. "Do you mean that I'm a bully?"

"We will raise our hands, for yes or no," Mrs. Chemsky said.

"I'm not," Mikey said.

"I think also we had better lower our heads and cover our eyes," Mrs. Chemsky said. "Yes, Justin?"

"Louis is fun, and I want him back in class," Justin said.

"Thank you, Justin."

"You have to admit you're bossy," Margalo whispered.

"What's wrong with that?" Mikey demanded.

"Quiet now," Mrs. Chemsky said. "Settle down. Everybody." She stared at Mikey. "Heads down, eyes covered? Raise your hand to vote yes or no, please, and keep it up until I tell you. All in favor —"

Hands shot up.

"Listen to the whole question, please, before you answer," Mrs. Chemsky said.

Hands were lowered quickly.

"All in favor," Mrs. Chemsky said, "of doing nothing, raise your hands." Mikey was peeking, and saw that nobody in the seats she could see raised a hand. But Mrs. Chemsky still waited a while, studying her own hands on the desk, before saying, "All right, now, all in favor of asking Mr. Delaney if Louis Caselli can return to our classroom?"

Mikey didn't have to look to see what she could hear. She'd have bet that twenty-nine hands went up. Ann Tarwell was absent that day, so that meant everybody was voting in favor. Even those people who weren't in favor probably voted yes.

"Hands down, then," Mrs. Chemsky said. "That looks like a clear decision to me. The next step is for me to talk with Mr. Delaney and the other teachers about reversing the decision. If," Mrs. Chemsky added, "Miss Elsinger will give us her word that there will be no more fisticuffs."

"But —" One look at Mrs. Chemsky's face stopped the words in Mikey's throat. "I promise I won't hit him first," she said.

That seemed to satisfy the teacher.

A swelling up of sounds started — a combination of pleasure at getting their own way from the teachers, and the sense that the world might be, after all, a fair place, whatever adults said.

Then Mrs. Chemsky's voice clanged down on them, like a door slamming in a movie about jail, or a TV show about jail. "Quiet. Everyone. Now. Take out your math homework, please."

When they talked about it at the end of the day, they all wondered, Would Louis Caselli be back with them, tomorrow? or after the weekend? Would having been suspended from school mean that Louis wasn't eligible to be class president, as he'd been most previous years? and Who was going to get the other three class offices? and How did Mrs. Chemsky's husband stand it, how strict she was?

Margalo had an answer for that one. "She doesn't have a husband," Margalo said, to Mikey and Karen and Ronnie. "You never hear about him, do you?"

"There could be a hundred reasons," Ronnie said. "They could be divorced. Or maybe he died. Is she old enough to have a husband who died in Vietnam?"

"She never had one," Margalo announced. "She just made one up, because it's easier to get a job if you're married, because then you can't get married and quit to go join your husband, wherever he is. That's why employers prefer married women," Margalo explained, and put her backpack over her shoulder, and left for her bus before anyone else could ask her any more questions.

Mikey couldn't help but admire Margalo.

The next morning, there he was, Louis Caselli. "Large as life," Margalo observed to Mikey. "Fit as a fiddle. Pleased as punch."

"She sure worked fast," Mikey said.

"She didn't like losing him, because it was a failure," Margalo explained. "So she wanted him back, because she didn't want some other teacher — Ms Spalding, especially, the way Ms Spalding teaches is much more permissive, very different — What if Ms Spalding could turn Louis into a good student? Mrs. Chemsky wants to be the one to do that."

Louis was the center of a bunch of excited people. They greeted him, and welcomed him back. Mikey and Margalo went to sit at their desks, and watch. Mrs. Chemsky was seated at her desk pretending that nothing special was happening.

"Is that something you know? or a rumor you're starting?" Mikey asked Margalo.

Margalo just smiled, as if she was the Mona Lisa.

"C'mon, Margalo. I know you start rumors."

"All right. I guess. OK. Then — it's my idea, but I bet I'm right. I bet she did want Louis back."

"Doesn't the expression on his face make you want to just punch him?" was Mikey's answer.

"Actually," Margalo said, "it makes me want you to punch him."

They both laughed, and Louis looked over to where they sat.

"Except I gave Mrs. Chemsky my word," Mikey said. She stared right back at Louis.

This was a big moment for the class. Godzilla meets King Kong.

Louis looked over at the teacher, and then back to Mikey, and he made his way over. He was smiling like some politician who really wanted them to vote for him. Mikey stretched out her legs, and smiled up at him, a NutraSweet smile.

"Louis," she greeted him, big smile.

"About your hair," Louis said, as if each word he spoke was some horrible bite of food he had to eat, as if he had just taken three bites of pickled squid. "I shouldn't," he said, two bites of boiled turnips.

"Have done that," he said, hurrying through three spoons of boiled egg with runny white.

Mikey almost liked the way he didn't say he was sorry. She started to like it but she stopped herself.

The whole class was watching.

"So, will you shake hands?" Louis asked.

Someone had told him he had to say this, and had to hold out his hand for Mikey to shake if she wanted to. His hard little eyes canceled out his smiling mouth, and she could see that somebody had told him he had to apologize, and shake, or else.

Louis's right hand was held out to her as if he wished it was a six-gun, a Colt .45, loaded and pointed at her, and his finger on the trigger.

Louis Caselli would be in heaven, if Mikey would just refuse to shake hands with him.

Mikey grinned her *I-see-through-you* grin, and her *I'm-about-to-seriously-win* grin. She stood up and thrust her right hand way out, and pumped his hand up and down, pumping hard, grinning away.

Louis said, "Don't think you're fooling me." He said it in a low voice, which he lowered even more to add, "Porky."

But he hadn't lowered his voice enough and Mrs. Chemsky heard him. "Louis," she said.

His face paled. He turned around to face her. "Yes, Mrs. Chemsky?" he said.

She stared at him. Ten seconds of staring. Twenty. Thirty.

He got paler. People backed away, and sat down in their desks.

"Tell me something, Louis," Mrs. Chemsky said. Then there was another five seconds of staring.

Louis was the only one standing. He didn't dare move.

"Yes, Mrs. Chemsky?" he asked.

Five seconds of staring before she asked, "How much do you weigh?"

"Ninety-one pounds," Louis said. "And a half," he added nervously.

"And Miss Elsinger? How much does she weigh? Do you know?"

"No, Mrs. Chemsky."

"She weighs ninety-three pounds," Mrs. Chemsky said. "Those are the weights on your two charts. Ninety-one-and-a-half, and ninety-three. So Miss Elsinger weighs about a pound and a half more than you do. She weighs about one large baking potato more."

"But she's much shorter than I am," Louis said.

"Excuse me. Excuse me, Louis, but I thought you were name-calling about weight. Not height."

"Yes, Mrs. Chemsky."

There was a ten-second stare.

"I won't do it again, Mrs. Chemsky."

"Do I have your word?

"Yes, Mrs. Chemsky."

"Does the class have your word, Louis?"

"Yes, Mrs. Chemsky."

"In that case, please return to your seat. We are late with attendance because of this."

By the time attendance was taken, and Rhonda — whose turn it was — had taken it to the office, and returned quickly to begin the Friday spelling test, and the spelling test had been taken and handed in, everything was back to normal.

During the last period, while they were giving their cubbies the Friday cleaning out, Mrs. Chemsky told them she had two announcements. The first was that they would be electing class officers next week, so she hoped they would start thinking about those votes. "Nominations on Wednesday morning," she announced.

The second announcement was that Activities would begin next week. Ordinarily, Activities would meet on Wednesdays and Fridays, but next week — because of the elections — they would meet Tuesday and Thursday. Activities came in six-week cycles, she reminded them, and their choices for this cycle were between: Model Building, Cooking, Reading Aloud to First-Graders, and Chess. While they were separating out used sheets of paper for recycling, and throwing away stubs of pencils, Mrs.

Chemsky called out their names in alphabetical order. In alphabetical order they told her what activity they wanted to sign up for and she put their names down on her list, under the proper heading. Old students were prepared for this and knew what their friends were choosing.

It was hard on Keith Adams, however, being new *and* having to choose first. "Chess?" he said, then looked at Noah, hopefully. Karen chose Cooking, which meant the Gap girls would all be doing that activity. Annaliese was sappy about little kids, probably because her divorced father had told her what a good mother she was going to make. She wore his picture in her locket and chose to read to first-graders.

Mikey and Margalo exchanged a look at that point, trying to figure out what they would say. Margalo thought reading to little kids might be fun but she didn't know that Mikey would agree.

Louis and Sal both chose Models; they already had their model kits, they said. Ronnie chose Reading Aloud, and Lee chose Chess, and Justin chose Models — He had a Wild Weasel, he told everybody, and smiled at Louis. Then it was Mikey's turn.

With an evil smile, the kind of smile when there is only one more spoonful of Ben & Jerry's chocolate chocolate chunk ice cream left, and you've had all the rest, too, but you're still not going to share, Mikey said, "Model Building, please."

"Models, too," Margalo echoed, although she couldn't match Mikey's smile.

"I have a palomino model," Mikey called across to Louis. "You know, the horse? With tack, and a jumping ring, too, I think. For my Barbie."

Louis's face was turning red.

"I've got Barbie at the Spa," Margalo announced happily, a major lie.

"Those aren't models, not for Model Building. You don't know *anything* about models," Louis protested.

"I know we don't," Margalo said, before Mikey could argue with him. "But you can help us."

"Is that really your choice?" Mrs. Chemsky wanted to know. "Miss Elsinger? are you sure? Margalo?"

"Oh, yes," they said. "Absolutely."

Louis looked like he might explode. He looked like a balloon with a face drawn on it and much too much air being blown into it.

But he didn't dare say anything.

And with perfect timing, the bell rang.

5

Who Wants to Be Class President?

On Monday morning, Mrs. Chemsky repeated her Friday announcement, with details. "This is the fifth week of school, the week we elect class officers for the year. President," she listed them in order of importance and even then, only one was out of alphabetical order. "Vice president, secretary, and treasurer. The class president will represent our class on the student council, and the vice president will fill in should the president be unable to attend a meeting. The secretary takes notes of what is said in class discussions — yes, Rhonda?"

"All of them? I thought it was just —"

"Just formal class meetings, that's correct. These are records of what is said and decided during a class meeting."

"Oh. That's all right then."

"I'm glad to hear that. The treasurer is responsible for the class funds. Yes, Justin?"

"Does he get to keep the money, now we're in fifth grade?"

"What do you mean 'he'? Who says it has to be a boy? A girl could be just as good."

"Yeah."

"Yeah."

"Better."

"Yeah."

"I didn't mean —"

"In any case," Mrs. Chemsky squashed that quarrel, "the actual money, the cash itself, is kept in a school account at the bank. The treasurer keeps the records, of how much money comes in, and from where, and how much money goes out, and for what purposes, and how much remains for the class to use."

"Oh, math."

"There will be a class meeting Wednesday morning to nominate candidates. Remember, nobody can run for more than one position. The elections will be held during sixth and seventh periods on Friday, during which time we will, first, hear the speeches, and then vote. Any questions?"

"We miss music?"

"Speeches? What speeches? We never had speeches before."

"Hot damn, we get out of music."

"Who has to give speeches? Mrs. Chemsky?"

"It is traditional in fifth-grade elections for at least one supporter for each candidate to tell us his, or her, reasons for preferring that candidate," Mrs. Chemsky said. "Yes, Louis?"

"Are there any rules about how if your behavior isn't perfect you can't be class president?" Louis Caselli wondered. "Like, if you've been to jail, you can't be President of the US?"

"Gee," Mikey said, "I wonder why he asked about that?"

"Don't start on me, Mee-Shell."

Mrs. Chemsky squashed their quarrel, too. "There is no rule to that effect, Louis," she said. "Do you want to suggest that Mr. Delaney should consider making one? No, I didn't think so. Are there any more questions?"

There were none. Mrs. Chemsky replaced the piece of chalk in the wooden tray below the chalkboard and dusted her hands together. She wore a plain gold wedding band, which everyone had noted, but no engagement ring.

What everyone didn't know was what it meant if a woman didn't wear an engagement ring. Some mothers didn't have them, and some did; of the mothers who were still married, that is. Divorced mothers, even if they still had their engagement rings, didn't wear them.

But the real question wasn't about whether or not Mrs. Chemsky should have an engagement ring. It was: What about Mr. Chemsky? Was there a Mr. Chemsky?

Those fifth-graders who had them reported whatever information they could gather from older brothers and sisters.

"She's thirty-five."

"She's forty-seven."

"Old enough to be married."

"Who says a woman needs to be married?"

"My mother says early thirties. My mother knows."

"She never brought him to school. Not even to chaperone a dance, at night, when she was a chaperone."

That morning, the curiosity about Mrs. Chemsky's marital status didn't distract her class — through social studies and language arts, and learning about the part the water table plays in the ecosystem — nearly as much as the curiosity about Who Might Be Class President?

"President's the only job that means anything," Mikey said. It was morning snack. Groups of people clustered together, eating snacks and discussing who would win.

Mikey's snack was a Granny Smith apple and some home-baked cheese twists, brown and crispy. Margalo wished she could have all of them instead of just the one Mikey offered. Margalo was snacking on a packet of finger cakes, bright fake strawberry pink with bits of coconut all over them, like white shaving hairs left in the sink. They tasted as good as they looked.

"A treasurer does something real," Margalo argued.

"We need to figure out who's likely to run," Mikey said. She opened her ring binder to a blank page and wrote at the top *ME*. She drew lines to divide the page into quarters.

Margalo did the same, except she put *Me* in the upper right corner, and she also titled each quarter — president, vice president, secretary, treasurer.

As they ate, they filled in names. Mikey put names in the top left-hand box: Tanisha Harris, Veronica Caselli, Keith Adams, Ira Pliotes. "I bet Ronnie gets tired of it always being Louis who gets elected," she said. "I would."

Margalo had two of the same names in her president box, Tanisha and Ira; then she had Justin, Lee, Malcolm Johnson, and Ann Tarwell. "It might be fun to have a girlfriend and boyfriend running against each other, wouldn't it? Like a TV movie. Do you think life should try to be more like TV?"

They filled in names and shared ideas. "The treasurer needs to be good at math."

"The secretary should have good handwriting."

"That means probably a girl. Besides, secretaries are always women," Margalo said.

"You mean, like the Secretary of State?" Mikey asked, sarcastic. "Secretary of the Treasury?"

Now what was bugging Mikey, Margalo wondered. Then she thought, she should have put Mikey down for something, if they were friends.

But — she took a peek — it wasn't as if Mikey had put her name down for anything.

But still.

She did think Mikey had leadership, the way people always said a class president should. Just, nobody would want to follow her.

That was the problem, sometimes, with people who had leadership. It just made the rest of the people angry.

Margalo thought about it, decided, and wrote Mikey's name down in the list for treasurer. Mikey was good at math.

Mikey watched her write. She wrote Margalo's name down for secretary, and then also in the box for vice president.

She looked at Margalo. Margalo studied the page before her.

Doodling, Mikey went over and over her own capitalized initials, at the top center of her paper, *ME, ME, ME.*

"I know that when people think what I'm like, secretary is the kind of thing they think I'm like," Margalo said, finally. "But I don't want to be a secretary. I want to be the boss. I know that there's something about the way I look —" she tucked her hair behind her right ear. "But my room's always a mess. Or, my part of the room is a mess. My sisters keep their parts neater."

"You share a bedroom?"

"With two of my sisters. Actually, one's a half-sister and one's a step. Not everyone can be an only child and have a room to herself. And not all of the mess in my part is only mine, if you want to be strictly honest about it," Margalo said.

"Do you have your own dresser? What about a desk, do you have your own desk?"

"We don't have desks."

"Bookcase?"

"It's not that bad." Margalo felt as if she had been whining, and complaining about her family, and criticizing. "I keep papers and things in one of my drawers. And we share a lot of stuff, clothes, and books, pencils. You know, sharing? Not keeping everything for yourself? Ever heard of it?"

"My mother says my room looks like twin bombs went off. One on each bed."

"You have two beds?"

"Twin beds. I got the twin beds my mother had in her room when she was little."

"If I had a room of my own, I'd keep it nice. I think. Do you have a desk?"

"Yeah. But — I hate housework. I hate chores, and I never do them, unless they threaten me with something terrible." Mikey smiled a Gingerbread Man smile, *Catch-me-if-you-can*, and added, "And they can't think of much that's terrible enough to get me to do housework."

"Although, I like ironing," Margalo said.

"You're kidding."

"No I'm not. It's peaceful. Besides, part of the reason my part of our room is so messy is, that way they can't find my stuff and go through it. You know? The way sisters always nose around in your stuff."

"Do you mean a diary? Do you keep a diary?"

"Not on your life. That would just be asking for misery."

"I'd never be able to stand having someone think they could go through my things. My parents know better than to do that. I'd throw a fit they'd never forget, not if they live to be a hundred. I'd — but, you know," Mikey admitted, "I do like washing the windows. I like the way the glass looks when it's really clean."

Maybe, Mikey was thinking, the reason why Margalo had never asked her over after school was because she thought her room wasn't nice enough, or her house, or her family. Unless, the reason was that Margalo didn't really like her personally, just liked her because there wasn't anybody else to be friends with in school, which would explain why Margalo only put her down for treasurer.

"You wash the windows? Inside and out? Even the upper stories?"

"We've got a modern house," Mikey said. "All on one floor."

Margalo was beginning to suspect that the reason Mikey hadn't asked her over might be shyness and secretiveness. Mikey didn't like people getting close, in Margalo's opinion. Margalo guessed, if she was the kind of person people got mad enough at to chop off her braid, she wouldn't be too trusting, either. Even if someone was her friend.

But if Mikey was her friend, why didn't Mikey think she'd be good for class president? What were friends for, if not to want their friends to be class president?

Somehow, by lunchtime, Margalo and Mikey were having a fight. They hadn't actually quarreled about anything, but they weren't friends at lunch recess.

Mikey went off to play soccer, walking away with Tanisha.

Margalo joined Ronnie and Annaliese and their friends at four-square, and they all talked about class officers. Actually, it wasn't talking so much as complaining. "Louis has been the president for years," Annaliese said.

"Was he less of a numbchuck last year?" Derrie asked. "I can't see how he ever got elected."

"Everybody always just voted for him," Annaliese explained.

"Not always. You were president in second grade," Ronnie pointed out.

Annaliese fingered her locket, and said she'd forgotten that.

"What did you do?" Margalo asked. "I mean, what was the job like?"

"I went to meetings and raised my hand when everybody else did," Annaliese said. "It was boring, you just listened to people talk and then voted. But it felt good, being *president*. My father boasted about me."

Doucelle was getting restless. "Everybody ready to start?"

Ann said, "There are more girls than boys in the

class. We could elect a girl president, if all the girls voted for her."

"What difference does being a girl make?" Margalo asked.

"Because they think they can run everything."

"But whoever it is can only be one thing or the other, boy or girl," Margalo said. "It doesn't make any sense to care if it's a girl or boy, since it *has* to be one or the other, since caring only means that you feel like you won or you feel like you lost. Which has nothing to do with *who* is president, who personally, not who a girl or who a boy."

There was a little hesitation while they tried to figure out what she meant. Doucelle threw the ball to Derrie, who caught it and held it.

"It's the principle of the thing," Ann said.

"My principles are about having someone for president who I think will do a good job," Margalo said. "Who were the officers last year? Besides Louis."

"Justin. Justin was the most popular boy in the class last year, wasn't he, Ann? Look, she's blushing."

"He still is," Ann said.

"Derrie? You awake?" Doucelle asked.

"I don't think so," Derrie said. "What about Malcolm? Or Keith, Keith is really cute, I think."

"Hey, c'mon, Derrie," Doucelle said, and clapped her hands. "Throw it here."

"Or Ira," Derrie said.

"Ira's ears stick out," Ann argued.

Margalo wasn't about to be distracted. "We were talking about class president."

"Why are you so interested?" Ronnie finally wondered.

"I'm new," Margalo said, which they all knew. "I've never had a class president before," she said, which was a lie.

"It doesn't matter who's president," Ann said. "Except for feeling popular, it doesn't make any difference, and it always works out even — there's a girl for vice president, a girl secretary, and a boy treasurer."

"They, you know, work together?" Denise added. "Plan dances? or bake sales? I was the secretary, in third grade. I had to bake millions of cookies, or anyway my mother did. The class officers have to be leaders and what that means is you get stuck volunteering all the time."

Doucelle said, "Are you going to throw it, or what, Derrie?"

"I'm going to or what," Derrie said.

"But what if there's something important?" Margalo insisted.

"Like what? We're kids," Ronnie reminded her.

"There still could be," Margalo said. "Like — I don't know — if somebody wanted to propose that — homework be abolished —"

"Who's doing that?" Derrie asked. "*I'll* vote for him."

"Or her. It could be a her," Ann said.

"Or to organize kids to work in a soup kitchen for the homeless," Margalo said.

"My father wouldn't let me," Annaliese objected.

"*Guys,*" Doucelle complained. "Are we playing?"

"Or anything new. I can't think of anything right now," Margalo said, "but you know the kind of thing I mean. Like roadside cleanups, bottle collections."

"Teachers take charge of important things," she was told.

Margalo gave up. "But if it doesn't matter," she asked, "why does everybody get so excited about it?"

The answers came quickly. "To show leadership." "Popularity." "It goes on your record?" "To be the winner." "To get out of class for student council meetings." "To sit on the stage during assemblies." "You're the president? and everybody knows." "It's the kind of thing parents really like you to do."

Doucelle gave up, too. "You all aren't even interested in this game. Are you?" and she ran off to the soccer field.

Being class president didn't sound to Margalo like that big a deal. She couldn't see why she shouldn't get elected. She would have liked to ask Mikey if Mikey thought she should run, but Mikey was in a mean mood. She made fun because Margalo left blank lines below each spelling word for the definitions, and numbered the words, and didn't have erasures. Mikey called Margalo "Miss Perfect Paper" and "Prissypencil," and smiled.

Margalo turned in her seat so she wouldn't have to see Mikey, even out of the corner of her eye, Mikey with her weird green hair that looked like previously owned vegetables, hair that looked like a compost heap. She ought to say that to Mikey, she thought and wrote down the next word, *oligarchy*, and skipped three lines, and numbered the next line, 8.

Mrs. Chemsky waited a minute, giving everybody time, before she said, "Parliament. Capital P," she started spelling out loud as she wrote the word on the board. "Are you going to copy this word, Miss Elsinger? Or has your spelling undergone a miraculous transformation overnight and you no longer need to pay attention when I am introducing the spelling list."

"No," Mikey said.

"No," in a warning voice, "what?"

"No, my spelling hasn't had a miracle."

She heard the muffled laughter and realized what the teacher wanted and didn't have the energy to disobey. "No, Mrs. Chemsky," she said. Mikey was busy being homesick for her old school. Here, everyone thought it was all right for the boys to be the only ones to have fights, or play soccer, or be class president.

Mikey had never settled for class vice president before, and she didn't see why she should begin now. *ME*, she wrote at the top of her paper. In her old school, they asked her if she wanted to be class president, and she said yes, so they all voted for her.

Not because she was popular. Mikey knew that. It was because she was the most — the most of everything, and if she wanted to be class president, then that was what she got. Margalo could be vice president.

Margalo was sitting with her back turned. Not very friendly, sitting with her back turned like that.

"Psst," Mikey hissed, as Mrs. Chemsky wrote *filibuster* on the board, slowly spelling it out. "Psss-ssst."

Margalo turned around, whispered, "What."

"Gotcha!" Mikey whispered.

"Girls," Mrs. Chemsky warned then both, but she was looking at Margalo.

Sometimes, Margalo wanted to punch Mikey in the nose, just the way Mikey used to go after Louis Caselli. In fact, if she'd known how to, Margalo would have punched Mikey right then; and not only would that show Mikey, but also Margalo would be the first fifth-grade girl sent to the office. Or maybe — this was a good, mean thought — she would nominate Louis Caselli for class president, and vote for him, too.

That would serve Mikey right. Because Margalo was willing to bet that Mikey wanted to be president. If Margalo sort of wanted it, she could be sure Mikey wanted it a lot.

And that made sense, too. It explained what was eating Mikey.

Now everything made more sense. "Shut *up*," she whispered to Mikey. "Later, OK?" she whispered and smiled placatingly at Mrs. Chemsky, and turned her attention to writing down on her list the tenth word, *compromise*. This was the election week vocabulary list, and pretty predictable.

Anyway, Mikey had simmered down, and stopped trying to pick fights during class. But she'd left the silent *e* off the end of *compromise*, and Margalo didn't tell her.

"You want to be class president, don't you," they accused each other, at the end of the school day.

"You first," Mikey said at the same time Margalo said, "You first."

"Well, sort of," Margalo admitted as Mikey said, "I guess so."

"Well, I *could*," they justified themselves. "I'd be good, as good as anyone else."

"Except maybe you," they added, not that they believed it.

"So, the question is, who wants it more?" Mikey asked.

"I do," she answered.

At that, Margalo lost it, completely lost it. "Wrong," she said and "Blaaat." She shoved at Mikey with her hip and shoulder, as if to crowd Mikey out of the spotlight, if they had been standing on a spotlit stage. "*I* want it," she said.

"Hey," Mikey said. "Don't do that."

"Don't do what, don't say I want what I want?" Margalo was overflowing with anger before she even noticed that her anger level was rising. She swung her hip and shoulder at Mikey again. "Or, do you mean: Don't want something you've decided you want?" She knew what Mikey actually meant; but she thought that the actually covered up a really, and it made her angry.

Mikey turned, and faced her, and pushed at her with both hands. Margalo stumbled backwards, but she didn't lose her balance. Anger was flowing up and out of her, as if she were Old Faithful or something. Or as if she was Mikey's hair, vomit-green anger shooting out from the top of a head. Margalo stuck her face right back at Mikey. "What do you think you're doing?"

"Just what you're doing."

"You can't push me around like that!"

"Oh yeah?"

Push.

"Says who?"

Push. Push.

"Says," shove, "me."

"Go ahead, hit me. Try it."

So Margalo did. A real punch, not a flail. Mikey blocked the punch with her arm. Margalo punched again, and got Mikey's cheek, with the bone under it, and that hurt. It *hurt* to hit people.

Then Mikey punched at her, hard. Mikey was better at fighting; Margalo wouldn't deny that. The punch caught her left shoulder, and then another fist was coming at her face, but Margalo ducked so Mikey just got her in the neck.

Margalo backed up.

She backed up into a desk, and Mikey was right on her.

Mikey was really good at fighting.

Margalo really wasn't.

Margalo used her legs to push Mikey away, off. The desk she was leaning against clattered over and Mikey fell down over another desk, backwards, and fell over onto it when it fell over, and Margalo didn't know if she should jump on Mikey and pummel, or stand back and see if maybe she'd won the fight.

Mrs. Chemsky was back in the room by then. "What are you two doing?" she demanded, in a voice like a foghorn. "What is *wrong* with you?" Mrs. Chemsky's foghorn voice demanded.

Margalo was glad Mrs. Chemsky had arrived on the scene.

"Nothing," she muttered. Her throat was too tight to say any more.

Mrs. Chemsky was hauling Mikey up by an arm, and Mikey looked like she was about to cry or something. Ha-ha on Mikey.

"I'm not picking up any desks," Mikey said. "It's all *her* fault."

"Not," Margalo said, pushing the word out of her stiff throat.

"Neither of you is picking up anything," Mrs. Chemsky said. "Neither of you is staying in this classroom for one minute longer. If you didn't have buses to catch, I'd tell you where you'd be going, but for right now I just want both of you out of my classroom, out of my sight, out of my hair. Out of my life for the day. Don't —" she was saying, but by then Mikey and Margalo were out in the hallway, running for the buses, running away from each other.

*　*　*

Mikey hoped that sleeping on it would make Margalo less stubbornly selfish. Or was it selfishly stubborn? Whichever, she came to school Tuesday morning hoping that Margalo would apologize and say, Of course Mikey should be class president.

On Tuesday morning Margalo thought and hoped the same, only reversed.

They neither of them said much of anything to each other.

Margalo, in fact, got into a conversation with Derrie and Doucelle about Mr. Chemsky, and what happened to him. "If there ever was one," Margalo said. They were whispering, their heads close together, and nobody could hear what they were talking about. "I don't think she murdered him. She doesn't seem like a murderer, because she's strict, but she's fair. Don't you think?" Margalo asked.

"It could have been an ugly divorce — like Burt and Loni — or she could be ashamed of him. If he's a drug dealer," Doucelle suggested. "My mother says it's none of our business. Or a terrorist fundamentalist something."

"How about if he's a terrorist fundamentalist drug dealer?" Derrie asked.

"It could be all just some rumor," Margalo suggested, in a low whisper, "and he's just some ordinary person with an ordinary job."

"Or something very sad, like he's in a coma on

life-support forever. Or in a mental asylum, forever," Doucelle said. "Mom's right, it isn't really our
business. Don't you think? Or he's a hostage somewhere."

Derrie said, "A hostage somewhere and nobody
knows? Not likely."

Meanwhile, Rhonda had come to talk with Justin
and Ann — who had been trying to figure out how
to get their parents to drop them off at the mall
on Saturday — about the class presidency. "You
should run," Rhonda told Justin. "People would
much rather have you than Louis."

Justin didn't know about that. Louis was his
friend.

Rhonda was certain, and she asked Ann to cor-
roborate her opinion.

Every now and then Rhonda looked around to
see who was listening.

Mikey pretended to be deaf.

"A lot of us think you'd be best," Rhonda said,
"and then if Ann was the vice president, that would
be good, don't you think? What do you think of
that? It sounds better than Louis and, if Louis was
elected class president, probably everyone would
want Mikey to be the vice, so it wouldn't look like
anyone was picking sides."

Justin thought Louis was thinking of having Ronnie for a vice president, and that would make Ron-

nie really happy. Rhonda reminded Justin that it wasn't as if Louis got to choose. There was voting, she reminded him. Justin thought Mikey could be secretary, but Rhonda knew better. "She'd hate that."

"What about Tanisha, anyway?" Ann asked. "Or Ira, or Lee? Or Keith, and he's new, too. Everybody should get a chance, that's what I think, not just the same people over and over."

Rhonda ab-so-*lute*-ly agreed with that.

"As long as it's not someone who'll — you know, make it embarrassing to have her for president, or have to get taken off the position because of fighting. Or something. I'd just be so *ashamed*," Rhonda said. She asked, "Wouldn't you?"

What decided Margalo was hearing Rhonda talk like that. "All right," she told Mikey. "You can do it, but next year I get to be the one who runs for class president. Will you promise that?"

"Sure," Mikey said. "Sure, promise. It's a smart idea. So how are you going to get people to vote for me?"

As if Margalo hadn't already been cross enough at Mikey, it turned out that Mikey hadn't been kidding about her horse model, except one horse model was in fact all she had. Two plastic pieces to glue together, and they'd have a horse for Barbie to ride.

"You really have Barbie dolls?" Margalo asked. "And Ken, do you have Ken, too. Cowboy Ken and College Ken? College Ken visits Malibu Barbie —"

"Lay off, OK?" Mikey interrupted. "My mother thought all little girls should have Barbies, and otherwise her little girl wouldn't be normal." She smiled, a bright, fake, normal little girl smile that became scary in about one second, without changing at all.

"I had one of the clone Barbies," Margalo admitted. All there was for them to do was glue the two horse halves together; then they could paint it if they wanted. Big whoopee. "The clones are cheaper."

"Barbie makes it easy to think of presents," Mikey griped, "if you don't want to think of what someone really wants and asked for."

Margalo said, "But all I did was give her a crew cut, and then we used her for operations for a while. Do you know what's inside those dolls?"

Mikey wasn't interested. She was setting out little bottles of paint, and two brushes.

Margalo wasn't interested, either. She wondered how Mikey would feel about a drooling contest.

At the other side of the room, the boys had pulled their desks together. They were talking, and laughing loudly, and separating the plastic pieces for their models. Mrs. Chemsky corrected the social studies workbooks at her desk, not wasting time while she had the job of supervising the model-making activity. Margalo thought about whether she *had* to get someone to second Mikey's nomination, and what would happen if nobody did. Anything was more interesting than this dumb horse of Mikey's, Margalo thought crossly. Even if she had to admit, in all fairness, that she was in the same activity as the boy she had a crush on. She had to thank Mikey for that, she guessed.

"I thought you said you had tack," Margalo complained. "A palomino with tack," she added. "And a jumping ring. I thought the Barbie part was the lie. This is going to take about one-half minute."

"Not if we go slowly."

"It's boring."

"I can't help that," Mikey said. "You can paint the head," she offered. "I just said whatever I thought would make Louis angry."

"How do you feel about a drooling contest?" Margalo asked. She poked a pin into the seal at the top of the little tube of glue. They each took a toothpick to spread glue on the edges of a horse half.

"A what? What's that?" Mikey asked. "To see who can drool more? Did anyone ever tell you how weird you are?"

Margalo sighed, as she watched Mikey press the two halves together. Mikey was watching the clock, timing for two minutes, and Margalo shifted in her desk, and sighed again.

She was going to *have* to vote for Mikey, and she was going to *have* to sit here being bored out of her skull during activities for six weeks, counting today, and all they got out of it was winning out over Louis Caselli. Sometimes, winning wasn't worth it. "You do the head," Margalo said. "I'll do the tail."

"Do you want the mane, too?" Mikey offered. This was so dumb, she didn't know how to begin being sorry she had gotten them into it. Maybe she should go ahead and play Margalo's drooling game.

"No, thanks," Margalo said. "I'm bad at painting. I'd ruin it. I'm bad at models, too."

"Who says?" Mikey demanded.

"I do. And my stepbrothers would agree with me." She didn't feel like talking about this. "I'm going to see what the boys are working on."

Mikey put down the horse and stood up with Margalo. "Me, too. But listen, I've noticed about brothers that they like to tell younger brothers and sisters they're no good at doing things."

"You don't have any brothers."

"But I've noticed. Sisters, too, but they're —"

"Sneakier. How do you know that?"

"Always criticizing, is what I was going to say. Like parents."

They moved across the room. Louis and Sal were

working together on a helicopter. Henry had a big aircraft carrier, and he needed two desktops to spread out all of his pieces. "Mine's skill level three," he greeted them proudly. He held up a round gray piece. "Remember the gun that exploded? on the Navy ship? and killed people? This is one just like it."

"Whyncha bring your model over to show us, Mee-Shell?" Louis asked. "Me and Sal have a Super-cobra, it's an A-H 1-T attack heliocopter. Twin jet engines," he said. "What've you got? Ours we'll be lucky to get finished in the twelve periods, even with two of us working on it. What's yours, a horse? But you're finished already. That's too bad," he said. Louis had cold, mean blue eyes. "Hey, man," he asked Justin, as if Mikey had suddenly turned invisible, "what's that?"

"F105G Wild Weasel," Justin answered, off-handed with pride.

"Oh wow," Margalo said. "That's really — I mean — that carries both the Shrike and the AGM-78 missiles. Doesn't it?"

Both boys looked surprised.

Sometimes, it was almost worth it having step-brothers.

"How do you know about . . . ?" Justin started to ask, but Louis kicked at the legs of Justin's desk, which scattered the model pieces Justin had set out.

"Cut it out, Louis," Justin said, and Louis kicked again.

Ira helped Justin pick up the pieces that had fallen onto the floor. Then he went over to the grocery bag in which he'd carried his Lunar Landing Module, with miniatures of Neil Armstrong and Buzz Aldrin, Jr., and the equipment they needed for the photographic missions and the scientific missions they were entrusted with. He pulled another model box out of the bag and offered it to Mikey. "I don't know if you'd like to try this. If it would interest you."

"What is it?" Mikey asked. She wanted to say yes, just because that would show Louis Caselli he couldn't boss everybody around. But she didn't know how Margalo felt about taking it.

"Thank you," Margalo said.

Ira said, "Probably it's too easy for you, but it's more fun than that horse. Do you have glue?"

"Yes," Margalo said. "I'd like to put a Klingon warship together. Wouldn't you, Mikey?"

"You mean Mee-Shell," Louis muttered, and Sal squeezed out a little laugh but he kept an eye on Justin, who wasn't pretending to find anything Louis Caselli said funny, and he kept an eye on Mrs. Chemsky who might come down on them like a ton of bricks at any moment, for any reason.

Mikey accepted the box from Ira and banged it

down flat on top of Louis's head. "Oh. Sorry. Slipped," she said, with a wide, nasty smile. A *You-got-a-complaint?* smile.

"Mikey," Margalo protested, and took the box, but Ira wasn't paying any attention to Louis and Mikey.

"We probably won't have time to paint it," Margalo said to him. She'd read quickly over the information on the box. Thirty-five pieces wasn't very hard. She'd never tried a model that simple. Thirteen inches long wasn't very big, and if the pieces were small, and delicate, there might be *some* hard parts. "We ought to get to work," she told Mikey.

"But Ira," Mikey protested. "This cost sixteen dollars. I'm not going to pay you for it."

"He didn't say we had to," Margalo pointed out.

"You don't have to paint it," Ira said, "because my little sisters love to paint things. My aunt gave it to me. You'd be doing me a favor if you put it together," Ira said. He had round brown eyes, like a dog, and his ears did stick out.

Both Mikey and Margalo knew it would be mean to thank Ira for being nice, so they just went back to their desks. They shifted the horse, lying on its side on a piece of newspaper, onto the floor, and forgot about it. Mikey opened the box and examined the parts, while Margalo read the directions.

"I can do this, I bet," Margalo said.

"*We* can," Mikey corrected her. "Of course we can. Why shouldn't we be able to? Give me those."

"In a minute. I'm not finished."

"Now."

Margalo lowered the unfolded directions, as if they were a newspaper, and looked at Mikey over the top of them like her stepfather at the breakfast table. "You can't boss me around like you can your other friends," she said.

Mikey's face got hard, just for a second, and then she smiled a mean little smile, which got pinched up as if someone was trying to force her to swallow that smile and she didn't want to, and then she laughed a short little laugh, like a dog's bark before someone muzzles him to silence, and then she asked her desktop, "What other friends?"

Margalo said, "Everybody you expect to vote for you."

"Oh, them," and Mikey smiled, a big fake toothy politician smile. "They're not friends, they're voters. They don't *have* to do what I want." She looked over at Margalo, then.

Margalo was sitting there drooling, staring right into Mikey's face while drool oozed out over her lower lip.

"You're good," Mikey said to Margalo. "But I bet I'm better."

6

And the Winner Is . . .

At the end of the day on Thursday, Mrs. Chemsky called her class to attention, asking them to pay good attention.

She reminded them that yesterday's nominations had been the first step in an orderly process, and that each nomination had been seconded by someone other than the nominator or the candidate, and that had been the second step. On Friday afternoon, for each office, starting with president —

"That's you, my man!"

Mrs. Chemsky called her class to attention. She advised them to settle down, since she didn't intend to raise her voice to be heard.

As she was saying, Tomorrow there would be time allowed for brief speeches of support, for each candidate. After a speech, any member of the class might add his or her own exhortation. Did they know that word, *exhortation?*

She called them to attention, and warned them that she was at the end of her patience.

Was everything, she inquired, clear?

"Yes, Mrs. Chemsky," every voice in the room affirmed.

Mikey used the time between the last bell and getting onto her bus to chase Margalo down and ask, "Have you been exhorting people?"

"What do you think I am, your slave?"

"Are you still angry? About me running? No," Mikey decided, "you're too sensible, you can't still be angry."

"Of course I am, you jerk." Margalo would have yelled it, if they'd been alone. But they weren't, so she had to speak in a normal voice. "What do you expect people to feel like when you boss them around?"

"I didn't think you'd try to make me lose, though," Mikey complained.

Margalo felt like kicking Mikey, kicking her hard. "Do you think I'm doing *that?*"

Mikey took the question seriously.

It was, also, a very serious question, especially if they were friends.

"No," she decided. "No, I don't think you would."

"Should I be flattered?" Margalo asked.

"Neither would I," Mikey said. "We both play fair."

Margalo could fight on, or give up. "OK, then," she said. Giving up.

Mikey realized, "I guess I'd feel sort of angry too, if you were the one who got to run. But what do you think, will I win? What are people saying?"

"Nobody talks about it to me, but — I don't see why not," Margalo admitted. Privately, Margalo was convinced that *she* would have had a better chance than Mikey to be elected president of the fifth grade. But she'd never say that. There were things she couldn't say to Mikey — like that she'd cost them the election, like that her hair looked like pea soup some cat had sat in.

Mikey also was wondering if Margalo wouldn't have had a better chance. Fewer people probably disliked Margalo than disliked her, she thought, but she wasn't about to admit that out loud.

Besides, they both thought and neither said, it was too late, anyway.

Rain fell heavily the next day, which was bad luck because it meant they couldn't play their first soccer game. It was worse luck because election day was a bad time for a class to be cooped up inside together, all day. But it was fun the way all the election excitement kept bouncing around the room, like molecules being heated up. In fact, there were some people — Mikey, for one — who preferred things heated up. The more chaotic things were, the more excited people were, she thought, the better her own chances of being elected.

"What a day," she said, but Margalo was talking to Ronnie.

"Are you going to make a speech about Louis?" Margalo was asking.

"You're kidding, aren't you? I'm voting for Mikey," Ronnie answered.

"Good," Mikey said.

"Can't you say thank you?" Margalo asked.

"Why should I thank her? I'm the best candidate."

"I didn't say *that*," Ronnie laughed. "I just said I was going to vote for you."

Knowing a good exit line, she cut through the clumps of people to return to her desk, before either Margalo or Mikey could answer that they hoped she'd be elected secretary.

The room was so noisy, and excited, that nobody noticed that Mrs. Chemsky had entered it until she knocked against Wesley Oates's desk. "Excuse me, Wesley," Mrs. Chemsky said.

Wesley and Harvey said Good Morning, Mrs.

Chemsky, and that alerted Ira and Ann and Malcolm and Lindsey to quiet down, and turn around. "Good morning, Mrs. Chemsky," they all four said.

Then they stared, because Mrs. Chemsky was carrying a suitcase.

Silence spread out, like spilled milk.

Mrs. Chemsky had never carried a suitcase to school before, not that year, not any time any other class had ever mentioned, or any older brothers and sisters, either.

Mrs. Chemsky continued to the front of the room and set the suitcase down beside her desk, where everyone could see it.

It was only an overnight case, not a real suitcase. It wasn't large enough for a long trip, but probably — they wondered and decided to themselves — Mrs. Chemsky was leaving right after school to go somewhere for the long Columbus Day weekend.

There was a tag stapled around the handle. Margalo leaned over to look between Karen and Joanna. "LHR," she read aloud.

"Do you know what that is?" Karen asked. She leaned away to the right to give Margalo a clear view.

"London Heathrow," Margalo said.

"What's Heathrow?" Joanna asked. She was leaning away to the left.

Mikey cut in. "An airport. In London. In England," she added without actually saying what she was thinking, which was, *Dummy.*

Mrs. Chemsky was opening the roll book, and maybe that was what made Karen and Joanna sit up straight again, and turn their backs to Mikey and Margalo.

"*I* know that, too," Justin put in from beside them. "You aren't so smart, Mikey. You just think you are."

"What —" Mikey started to ask him what was so smart about knowing that London was in England, but "Keith Adams," Mrs. Chemsky called in a sharp voice, and the class came to attention.

"Here," Keith answered.

Mrs. Chemsky was wearing a red blazer, with a silver weird animal pinned on her lapel, maybe a weird dog, maybe a weird dragon, unless it was a silver mashed VW bug and not an animal at all. She wore a white lacy blouse. It wasn't unusual for her to wear dark trousers, but the blazer, and the pin, and the lacy blouse were not what her class was used to. Mrs. Chemsky looked fancy, and not as old as usual.

"Yes, Louis?" Mrs. Chemsky said.

"Are you going away?"

"Yes, Louis. It's a holiday weekend. Yes, Rhonda?"

"Where are you going?" Rhonda asked.

"I think that's my private business, don't you?" Mrs. Chemsky said. "Yes, Rhonda?"

"I was only asking."

"Karen Blackaway," Mrs. Chemsky said.

"Here," Karen answered.

"Joanna Burns. Yes, Joanna?"

"Does LHR stand for London Airport?"

"Yes, it does."

"I just wanted to be sure."

"What do you say, Joanna?"

"Oh. Sorry to interrupt."

"That wasn't what I was asking," Mrs. Chemsky said. "But thank you, your apology is accepted. Now, what do you say?"

"Oh," Joanna said. "Here," she said, "sorry."

"Louis Caselli," Mrs. Chemsky said and "Here," Louis answered, and the class settled down, despite elections, despite Mrs. Chemsky being dressed up and with a suitcase, despite Mikey's hopes.

The morning went by. Slowly. Outside, rain raced down the long windows. All at once, everyone in the classroom knew that summer was really over, good and over, over for good. In summer, fat warm drops rained down straight. This was a cold, slanting October rain. They were really in school for the year. Light years in the future, next May, they could begin to look forward to enjoying themselves again.

But for now, they guessed, they'd just have to get to work.

If any of them had looked, they would have seen Mrs. Chemsky smiling to herself as she calmly called out spelling words — *constitutional* — and waited for the sound of pencils moving over paper to end before calling the next word — *amendment*.

During recess, for which Mrs. Chemsky allowed the special privilege of ten extra minutes, five at the beginning and five at the end, the talk in the classroom grew excited again. There was excited talk about the elections coming up after lunch, who was speaking for whom, who was voting for whom, who had what to say about which candidates for which position. There was excited talk about Mrs. Chemsky, and whether or not she had in her suitcase — as Noah and Sal were maintaining — some piece of her murdered husband, which she would bury in some distant woods. "Maybe some woods, like, in England," Sal said. "They'd never connect a finger in England, or an ankle, or just some part of the body, with here," Noah said. "She could get a whole thigh in there, don't you think?"

"Maybe he just has a job in another part of the country, like a lot of couples," Hadrian Klenk suggested reasonably. "And she's going to visit him. It's a holiday," he pointed out.

"What do *you* know, nerd?" he was asked and he

was told, "More likely, maybe she's visiting him in some institution. Where he's crazy."

"In drug rehab, or in jail and if anyone finds out she'll be fired."

"She's been teaching here for years, stupid."

Lindsey maintained that Mr. Chemsky was just a made-up person. "My aunt wears a wedding ring and she's not married. She wears it to keep men from making passes at her."

Derrie dismissed that possibility. "Your aunt isn't everybody."

Rhonda said she'd asked her mother —

"You *didn't*," she was told. "How *could* you be so dumb?" she was asked, and, "What are you trying to do, get Mrs. Chemsky in trouble?"

Well, she'd already done it and besides, nobody had told her it was some big secret, and what was so wrong with her asking, didn't they want to hear what Mrs. Ransom had to say about Mrs. Chemsky?

"No," they said. That was a lie, but they had a point to prove.

Also, they knew Rhonda would tell them anyway.

However, before Rhonda could report what her mother had said, Mrs. Chemsky called the class to order again, and announced that the soccer game had been postponed, and announced that they would have math work now. "Take out your homework, and your math books, please," she said.

*   *   *

The feeling during lunch was that Louis Caselli would be elected for yet another year. His particular friends — Sal, and Justin, Clark, David, and Harvey — were exuberantly punching one another, and shoving one another, and Louis, too. Tanisha tried to get Clark and Harvey away from Louis's side, arguing that since they were all African-Americans they should all vote the same, but Clark just answered, "Then you should vote for our man, Tan."

The rest of the class could only hope that in junior high things would be different. Everybody assumed things this year weren't going to be any different because they couldn't be.

Except for Mikey. "I'm going to vote for who I like best," she said. "I'm going to vote for who I believe in. I'm going to vote for me, and you'd be smart to do the same," she said, to anyone who would listen to her.

"Not too modest, are you?" Derrie asked and "What good does modesty do?" Mikey asked and "You are so *bad*," Derrie said.

"Does that mean you're voting for me?" Mikey asked.

She knew she was speeding out of control. She wasn't stupid. She was going along too fast because she didn't dare slow down. It was like on the soccer field: Sometimes, you just couldn't think because if you did you might make a mistake. So she rolled along, too fast, just asking people over and over, "You really *want* Louis Caselli for your president?"

She concentrated on not smiling, because she didn't have a *Vote-for-me-you-won't-be-sorry* smile. She wasn't a real politician.

And when Margalo made whatever speech she was going to make, Mikey figured Margalo would say the kind of thing that would make people want Mikey to win the election. Mikey had a lot of faith in Margalo.

But at that moment, Margalo wasn't interested in the election. She was worrying about Mrs. Chemsky's invisible husband.

What Rhonda's mother had said was: She was going to get at the truth of this story. Because Rhonda's mother didn't want any bad influences teaching her daughter. She didn't want any questionable influences, either, or any influences with secrets which were probably shameful otherwise why were they being kept secret. Mrs. Ransom had a nose for trouble, and she knew a bad smell when her nose for trouble smelled it out. When Margalo heard that, she was almost sorry she'd started up on Mrs. Chemsky about the husband.

Almost, nothing; she *rea*-lly wished she hadn't.

But there wasn't much she could do, at this point, to undo the damage.

"Except for the wedding ring, I'd bet she's divorced, don't you think?" Margalo suggested to Ann Tarwell, after Rhonda's news. "What if he left her, to marry someone else, so she doesn't want to give up the ring because she still loves him."

"That is so sad," Ann sighed. "I couldn't stand that. Poor Mrs. Chemsky."

"Or because it's harder for a divorced woman to get a job, or get credit from banks," Margalo said. She knew from her mother's personal experience that that was true.

"Isn't that against the law?" Doucelle asked. "Isn't that discrimination? What do they expect women to do?"

"Anyway, I don't blame her," Margalo announced.

"Even if she just made up a husband and never had one? Even if she's been lying all along, to everyone?" Denise asked.

"I don't blame her," Margalo maintained.

"But she's so strict, and she has no right to act as if she's so perfect," Annaliese argued.

"And where's she going for the weekend? And why won't she tell us?" Linny wondered.

"Maybe it's private," Margalo said. If she were brave, she would tell them all — and after that it would take about five seconds for word to spread around the classroom and back to Mrs. Ransom — that any rumor about Mrs. Chemsky's husband had been started by her, Margalo. Started on purpose, just for fun.

Margalo was glad nobody except Mikey would ever guess her role in this. She knew Mikey wouldn't rat on her. She had a lot of faith in Mikey.

Everybody knew it was just a fifth-grade class election, and not worth caring about. Everybody cared about it anyway. All the parents and teachers and older sisters and brothers said it was just a fifth-grade class election, but they didn't know. It was important, who won and who lost, who got elected and who didn't. Because the person who won would be president, all year. And everyone would know who the losers were.

Finally, lunch recess ended. Mrs. Chemsky stood up and wrote on the chalkboard, in the upper left-hand corner, *president*. Then, in the middle of the board she wrote down the names of the four nominated candidates, in alphabetical order.

Mrs. Chemsky was the one non-fifth-grader who took this election seriously. "Louis Caselli," she wrote. Louis had been nominated by Justin and seconded by Salvatore, each one in position, like members of The Dream Team, like Johnson and Jackson

and Bird on a 3–2 break. "I nominate," said Justin.
"Second it," said Sal and "I accept," Louis finished.

"Michelle Elsinger," Mrs. Chemsky wrote. Margalo had made the nomination, and then waited to hope that someone would second it. Or maybe she hoped no one would. She wasn't sure how she felt. But Tanisha had quickly seconded it, so that was no problem.

"Sharon Huff," Mrs. Chemsky wrote, because the Gap girls had their own candidate this year, nominated by Karen and seconded by Lindsey. Mikey counted those four votes as goners, and wasn't even trying for them.

"Ira Pliotes," Mrs. Chemsky completed the list. Annaliese had nominated Ira, causing a buzz of speculation and alarm. Were they going together? Did Ira know she was going to do this? What did it mean, if a boy had a girl nominate him, was that better than another boy nominating him? Or not? But it was Henry — Henry! volunteering to speak! — who seconded it.

When all four names were listed on the board, Mrs. Chemsky turned around to look over her class. The air practically shimmered with nervousness and excitement. Mrs. Chemsky pulled down on her blazer, to straighten it. She said, "At this time, we will hear speakers for the candidates. Speakers, do not ramble on or I will cut you off. Understood?"

"Yes, Mrs. Chemsky."

Sal was the first to speak. "Stand up, Salvatore," Mrs. Chemsky told him, and he did as he was told.

Sal said, "Louis has always been the class president. Or almost always. He knows how to do it and he hasn't done a bad job, has he? So vote for Louis." He concluded with a joke. "Or he'll get you."

"Don't say *that*," Louis complained. "Stupid."

"Who're you calling stupid?"

"We have a secret ballot anyway, so nobody knows who you vote for," Harvey pointed out.

"I'll tell you who's the stupid one."

"Does anyone else have something to say about Louis's candidacy?" Mrs. Chemsky inquired. "Yes, David?"

"Louis is my man," David said, as he stood up. "I don't want any girl for my president, and I don't want anybody a girl wants to nominate, and neither does anyone else. So that leaves Louis."

"Thanks, David. Thanks a whole lot."

"But it's true, and you said so, too," David protested. "Yesterday. At recess. You *did*, Louis."

Mrs. Chemsky cut that quarrel off. "Anyone else?" There was nobody else who wanted to speak about Louis, so she called on Margalo, to speak for Mikey.

Margalo stood up.

"The thing about Mikey," Margalo said, and swallowed.

They were all looking at her and not very many of the faces were smiling. She concentrated on Tanisha's friendly face.

"The thing about Mikey," she said again, and ignored whatever it was that Louis was muttering, "is that she isn't afraid to say and do what she means. Mikey does what she wants."

"This is why I should vote for her?" Louis turned to ask Sal. "Because she doesn't care what anyone else wants?"

"Mikey," Margalo said, "gets things done. She doesn't just talk. Like, getting girls onto the soccer team."

That was her best point, so she ended with it.

Rhonda's hand flew up as Margalo sat down. "Yes, Rhonda?" Mrs. Chemsky asked, sounding as surprised as most of the class felt.

Rhonda stood up, and looked right at Mrs. Chemsky. She didn't look at anyone else. She put her hand over her heart to show how sincere a person she was and said, "I think people who are thinking of voting for Mikey because they feel sorry for her, on account of Louis and her hair? I think they shouldn't. Nobody likes her. They just feel sorry for her."

"I don't feel sorry for her," Louis muttered.

"Sit. Down. Rhonda."

Nobody could think of what to do next.

Everybody just wanted to pass on, and get the horrible moment over with. Everybody was embarrassed at Rhonda. She shouldn't have said that. You didn't say things like that in a class speech. Everybody thought of voting for Mikey, maybe; even Margalo thought of it.

Mikey sat like a stone statue at her desk.

At last, Mrs. Chemsky spoke again. She asked, Who was going to speak for Sharon Huff? And Lindsey Westerburg stood up to say, "I like Sharon, she's nice, she'd make a nice president," and then Lindsey sat down as quickly as she could, and Rhonda's nasty moment was behind them.

They didn't know if Annaliese would speak for Ira, and they were all relieved when it was Malcolm who raised his hand. Malcolm was the tallest boy in the class, and he had huge feet, and huge hands. He was planning to get a basketball scholarship to college, to get drafted into the pros right after college, because he was tall and African-American, and the best basketball player at WSE, best by a mile, he said, best by a mile and a half. "Ira's fair," Malcolm reminded them. "He's smart and he's fair — and he cares about if he's fair, too. I think those are," and he rolled out the phrase as if he'd been practicing it all night, "true presidential qualities."

Hadrian Klenk raised his hand. "Ira's friendly to everyone," Hadrian sat down, red-faced, and then stood right up again. "He's helpful."

Ira's ears were as red as Hadrian's cheeks, Margalo noticed. She still didn't dare look at Mikey.

"All right, then," Mrs. Chemsky said. "Put your heads down, class, cover your eyes. We'll vote now for the office of class president."

There was a brief delay, as if Mrs. Chemsky checked to be sure everybody's head was down before she called out, "Louis Caselli." Mrs. Chemsky's pencil scratched. "Michelle Elsinger," she called, and wrote, then "Sharon Huff," she called, and finally "Ira Pliotes." "Any abstentions?" Mrs. Chemsky's voice asked, but she didn't write anything. "You may raise your heads now," she announced.

They looked around, feeling foolish, then looked at their teacher.

"I am pleased to announce," Mrs. Chemsky said, "that Ira Pliotes is your class president for this year. Congratulations, Ira."

There were twenty-seven pleased faces, and many voices saying "congratulations," and "all right, Ira."

Mikey sat in her chair and concentrated on her

desk. She knew that when you peeked, and saw what you weren't supposed to see, you often saw what you wished you hadn't.

She wished she hadn't.

She had seen — peeking under her raised arm — that Margalo didn't even vote for her. Moreover, Mikey knew that it had taken barely longer to count her votes than it had taken to count however many votes Sharon Huff had gotten. Which was maybe one, if Sharon voted for herself.

She wished she hadn't said she wanted to be elected class president. She wished everybody didn't know she'd wanted it. She wished she could be in Margalo's position. Nobody knew that Margalo wanted it, too.

Mikey figured, although she hadn't had the heart to peek and find out, that Margalo voted for Ira. She didn't think Margalo would vote for Louis, and she knew Margalo's opinion of the Gap girls. But maybe she didn't know anything about Margalo. Because she had really believed Margalo would vote for her, and want her to be president.

Sometimes, Mikey almost couldn't stand how lonely it was.

Harvey was elected vice president, and Tanisha was elected secretary, which disappointed Ronnie so much she had to ask to be excused. Everybody knew how much Ronnie had wanted — just once — to be a class officer; but more people wanted Tanisha.

So she had won that one, at least, Mikey thought to herself. Thinking that was like sucking on lemons. Her smile got tight, and wrinkledy, an *Eat-prunes* kind of smile. Well, at least, she'd gotten a new smile out of this, Mikey thought, smiling away in the wrinkledy way until she got the feel of it and knew she could put it on, any time she wanted to.

There were only two nominees for treasurer, Keith Adams and Lee Cheung, two of the good math students. Mikey was better at math than either of them, and she wondered — now, when it was too late — if she wouldn't have been smarter to run for class treasurer. She'd had no chance at president, and she hadn't even known it.

She was so angry at Margalo that she couldn't even look at the girl. Her ex-friend. She was so angry at all of them that she couldn't look at anyone.

At the start of speeches about Lee and Keith, and who was the best candidate in whose opinion, Ira raised his hand. Mrs. Chemsky called on him. "Yes, Ira?"

"There are only two nominees," Ira said.

"Good counting, Prez," Louis Caselli said, sarcastic.

Ira ignored him. "Can I nominate someone else?"

Mrs. Chemsky's face filled with doubt. "May I,"

she said. Mrs. Chemsky had rules for elections: No more than four candidates for each office, All nominations made on the Wednesday before election, Nobody running for more than one position, All heads down during the voting.

"*May* I nominate someone else?" Ira asked.

Before anyone could start on an objection or agreement, Mrs. Chemsky raised her hand, and left it up. She wanted to think, silently. Mikey didn't care what happened now; let all the rest of them care if they wanted to. Besides, Mrs. Chemsky always kept her rules.

"Yes, you may," Mrs. Chemsky said to Ira.

Everybody was surprised, and so was Mikey. And she couldn't shut her brain up before it hoped that Ira was going to nominate her.

"I nominate Veronica Caselli," Ira said.

"Second it," Margalo hissed at Mikey.

Who did Margalo think she was hissing at?

"We've got a president who nominates *girls*," Louis moaned.

"Quick," Margalo insisted.

What made Margalo think she could tell Mikey what to do?

"Maybe I'll ask to get put back into Ms Spalding's class, if we've got a president who nominates girls," Louis complained.

"She's your *cousin*, Louis. Just shut up, OK?"

Margalo's hand shot up.

"Yes, Margalo?"

Margalo glared at Mikey.

"Who're you telling to —" Louis demanded.

"C'mon, Louis," Sal said. "Lay off for once."

"Yes, Margalo?" Mrs. Chemsky said again.

"Mikey wants to say something," Margalo said.

Thanks a lot, Margalo, thanks really a lot. But Mikey knew a barrel when she was over it, so she just said, "I second it."

Mrs. Chemsky nodded her head, and turned to add Ronnie's name to the list of candidates, between Keith and Lee. Mikey heard people murmuring. She couldn't help hearing what they were saying. "Way to go, Ira," she heard. "She can't be all bad, I guess." But Mikey didn't know if that last murmur murmured about her or about Mrs. Chemsky.

Mikey was glad now that she had seconded Ira's nomination.

Mikey had never really understood what TGIF meant, before. But that day there was nothing she wanted to do more than have school be over, and go home, and go into her room, and close the door, and get into bed, maybe with a bag of potato chips, and watch *101 Dalmatians* for maybe the five-thousandth time. And then watch it again.

Of course, Ronnie was elected. If Keith and Lee

felt less glad than the rest of the class about it, they were good sports. Margalo watched the way they looked at each other, shrugged, grinned. Sometimes, Margalo thought boys knew better than girls what was important. At that point, she couldn't wait to get out of school, and off the bus, and she would run herself a hot tub, and take a Coke into the bathroom with her, and one of the *Sweet Valley High* books from the pile of library books by her bed. She'd just read in the tub until she could forget. She knew Mikey was angry at her, but she didn't know why.

Because of having elections instead of math class, they got started a little early on the Friday cubby-cleaning chore, so they were ready to be dismissed five minutes before the bell would ring.

"You could let us out early," Louis Caselli suggested, when Mrs. Chemsky announced that they should sit quietly at their desks.

"I don't want to do that," she told him.

"We'd all like you," he offered.

At that, Mrs. Chemsky smiled. Many people saw it.

Then there was a knock on the classroom door, a man. He opened the door and stepped into the classroom. He wore a khaki suit, and a striped shirt — white stripes on a light blue background —

and a wide blue tie, with stars and a moon on it. He had a square jaw and shortish brown hair, getting a little thin at his forehead. He had a short thick nose, and he seemed pleased to see Mrs. Chemsky.

"You're early." Mrs. Chemsky sounded uneasy.

What a day, Margalo was thinking. What a day! Before she thought, she turned to smile at Mikey.

Mikey was waiting in ambush for her, with a thin-lipped smile that Margalo couldn't tell if it was about meanness or misery. Mikey's smile scared Margalo. She turned away.

"It's —" Mrs. Chemsky was looking at the clock on the wall. "There are still three minutes until dismissal."

"Oh. I've interrupted." The man had a low voice, sort of rumbly. "I'm sorry. Should I wait outside?" He had thick eyebrows and little light brown eyes.

Margalo would have liked it if he had been handsome.

"Yes, please, but wait. Steve? Let me introduce you. Class, this is Steven Chemsky."

They were already turned around, staring. "Hey," he greeted them, and vaguely waved the hand that wasn't holding on to the doorknob. "How's it going," he said to all of them.

"Hello," voices said, and "Hi." "Nice to meet you, Mr. Chemsky."

Then everything was quiet, for just five or ten seconds.

Of embarrassment for everybody.

"Well, I'll wait for you outside," Mr. Chemsky said, and Mrs. Chemsky sort of mumbled, "Fine. Good," and he left the room.

Her class stared at her.

She stared right back at them.

The bell rang. Mrs. Chemsky picked up her suitcase and was the first out the door into the hall.

The class burst into voice. "Wait'll I tell —" "— way he looked —" "I guess that —" "— that granola-people tie —" "How old —?"

Under all of the voices, Mikey let Margalo know just where they stood. "You didn't vote for me."

Margalo blew up. "Is that all you care about, the stupid election? What about Mr. Chemsky?" She was angry right back, now that she knew what it was about; even though she did feel bad for Mikey, hearing what Rhonda said; even though she was afraid Mikey disliked her, Margalo, personally and a lot, and so Margalo didn't have a real friend anymore; even though she agreed she maybe should have voted for Mikey even though she didn't want to. It was easier just to get angry.

"You said you would," Mikey grumbled.

"I never did. If you punch me, Michelle Elsinger, you'll be in big trouble, because you gave your word, in case you've forgotten. And," Margalo said, "I'll fight back, and I'll probably lose but I don't care, and I won't ever care about you again, no matter how many times you hit me. So go ahead, if you want to."

Mikey really wanted to. When Margalo called her Michelle, too.

"Who *did* you vote for?" she demanded.

"My vote is private. First you yell at me for not voting the way you want me to, and then you tell me I should tell you my private vote? Who do you think you are?"

"I'd have voted for you," Mikey said.

"You wouldn't even let me *run*." Margalo had never let herself get so mad before. She was practically enjoying herself, except she wanted to cry.

Not *true*, Mikey wanted to say. I'm *not* bossy, she almost said.

Margalo kept on quarreling. "Did you ever ask me who I *wanted* to vote for? Did you ever even *ask*? No. No, you didn't. You just yell at me for not doing what you tell me."

Mikey didn't dare open her mouth, for fear of what she might hear herself saying. If she'd been a running-away-from-trouble kind of person, she'd be running right now. Running away from this whole horrible afternoon.

Margalo figured it out. "You peeked! Didn't you!

That's how you know, isn't it?" Margalo hadn't dared to peek, to find out what the numbers were like, or who — for example — voted for Louis Caselli, or if anyone didn't vote for Ronnie to be treasurer. She would have liked to know those things. She almost admired Mikey.

Mrs. Chemsky would have gone ballistic if she'd caught Mikey peeking. That would have been a *won*-derful scene. It would have been a ter-*rific* end to the week.

"It's really cheating, to peek," Margalo said.

"Big whoopee," Mikey said. "Anyway, I know who you voted for, so don't act like it's such a big secret. Ira."

"How do you know that?"

"It makes sense."

"You are such a cheater —"

"I am not. *Not.* He's who I would have voted for if I hadn't voted for myself."

"Did you really vote for yourself?"

Mikey didn't feel like being told something else she did wrong.

"You're not supposed to vote for yourself," Margalo told her.

Let stuck-up perfect Margalo feel that way, if she wanted to, like some judge who knew all the right answers. "Who cares?" Mikey asked. "It's none of your business, anyway, unless you're the only one who gets to keep her vote private."

Margalo picked up her bookbag and hung it over her left shoulder. "OK. You're right about that," she said. "And OK. I know it hurt your feelings if I didn't vote for you. I can understand that and I'm sorry." Margalo squeezed out an apology as thin as the last bit of toothpaste from a tube. She never won fights, anyway. She didn't know why she even tried fighting, because all she did was lose.

"OK," Mikey said. "Why'd you vote for him, anyway?" she asked. "Instead of me." Not that she cared. Not that she wanted to hear the answer. But it was either ask that or think about whether the only person in class who liked her had given up on her.

"Because. Because he's nice. There's so much meanness this year — maybe fifth grade is a really mean year. Do you think?" That was as close as Margalo could come to saying what she was thinking — about how she wanted Mikey for her friend, but not if she had to be some slave; about how she didn't think she'd been such a great friend to Mikey that afternoon and she was afraid maybe she'd lost something she wanted to keep.

"You're mean, too," Mikey pointed out.

"But not in a mean way," Margalo said.

"That doesn't make sense."

"Yes, it does." Margalo stared right into Mikey's eyes, as if daring Mikey to say that what made sense to Margalo wasn't allowed to make sense. "And neither are you, mean in a mean way," Margalo said. "You just always want your own way no matter what." *So there,* she thought. "And your hair looks like a bowl of pea soup," she said. "That a cat sat in."

As soon as she finished, Margalo was already sorry. She *knew* better. She *knew* what happened when you said what you really thought.

"Boy are you weird," Mikey said. She wanted to start fighting again, except she didn't want to fight with Margalo. She tried to think about something other than the election to talk about as they walked to their buses. "What about Mr. Chemsky? He was pretty cute. For an older man, didn't you think?"

"That'll sure stop the rumors," Margalo said. She could barely grab onto her own thoughts. "But I wouldn't say he was cute."

Yes he is, Mikey wanted to tell Margalo, but she stopped herself. What she said was, "You wouldn't?"

"Well," Margalo said, so sarcastic that Mikey felt a surge of energy, enough energy to get angry with, "I just didn't."

They didn't even say good-bye, or see you. They didn't even wave a hand. Neither looked at the other to notice that she wasn't being looked back at. Both grunted — "Ghunnh."

A grunt wasn't a quarrel and it wasn't an apology and it especially wasn't a promise to try to change. A grunt wasn't a punch in the nose, either, and it wasn't the last thing to say before you never spoke again. A grunt was — like — a door cracked open: You can come in if you want to, I can come out if I want to, but I'm not asking. A grunt was just enough noise to keep contact, if anyone was interested in keeping contact.

"Ghunnh," Margalo said, and went to join Derrie in her bus line.

"Ghunnh," Mikey answered, moving away fast.

7

Nobody Likes You
Everybody Hates You

Because it was Columbus Day weekend, school didn't start until the next Tuesday. By that time, much of the excitements and disappointments of the elections had faded away; much, but not all.

Mikey met up with Margalo by the cubbies on Tuesday morning as they unpacked lunches and books. Margalo didn't say anything.

Mikey said, "We went to see *Apollo 13*. Have you seen it?"

Margalo shook her head. "Usually, we wait for the video."

"Are you still angry?" Mikey asked.

"What do you expect?"

Mikey had never thought to expect anything. She

had thought, friends voted for friends. She had thought it was simple.

She still thought that.

But she guessed Margalo didn't.

She gave Margalo a look at her new wrinkledy smile, *Eat-prunes.*

So they ignored each other. During morning recess, Margalo hung out with Ronnie and Derrie and Doucelle, leaning against the steel tubes of the jungle gym out front, and talking, as lazily as if it was summer, and they were all lying on some beach on some sunny day, all half asleep, talking. It was talk about the hamburgers at fast-food places, and whose family liked which hamburgers best, and whether they agreed with their families. It was nothing important, but it felt good to Margalo, a lot better than feeling bad about Mikey.

Mikey stayed inside during morning recess. She went to the school library to find a book to read, or to finish her math homework, or maybe just to talk to the librarian about what was new. The librarian thought Mikey was smart — which she was — and liked to read — which she did — and liked talking about books, which she didn't. Some days, however, it didn't hurt to try to think what it was she had liked about the newest Virginia Hamilton. Usually what she liked was a main character who didn't take any stuff off anyone. And was the opposite of popular. But still had feelings. And was the most interesting person in the book.

It was Tanisha who dared to ask, as they were taking out sheets of paper to write a three-paragraph essay about the growth of the railroads, "Did you have a nice weekend, Mrs. Chemsky?" This broke Mrs. Chemsky's rule about personal questions.

"Yes, thank you, we did," Mrs. Chemsky said and broke it right back. "Did you?"

Tanisha wasn't fazed. "Yes, ma'am, there were some high old good times at my house."

"I'm glad to hear that," Mrs. Chemsky said, turning to the board and beginning to draw a map.

"High?" Louis Caselli asked.

"What kind of high?" Justin wondered.

"Twerps," Tanisha responded. They couldn't get her going.

Mikey practiced spelling that word, after she had put her initials — *ME* — two lines tall, at the top of her paper. *Twurp, twirp, twearp, twerp — cherp,* Mikey wrote, and *perp*.

Slurp, burp, Margalo's hand wrote on her own paper.

Mikey let her mouth turn up at the corners, where Margalo could see it.

She wasn't going to kid herself. She was happier if Margalo wanted to be friends. This could be Margalo's way of saying that she wanted to be friends more than she wanted to be angry. Mikey guessed she felt the same way.

For lunch Mikey had a meatloaf sandwich, with provolone, mustard and mayonnaise, on the rye bread her mother brought home from a delicatessen near the office. "Want half?" she asked Margalo. "It's my favorite."

"Then I shouldn't. I just have bologna, with mustard." Margalo held the half sandwich she was eating out, to show Mikey. "On supermarket white. Nobody's favorite."

"We should. I want to," Mikey said.

"We should because you want to?" Margalo asked.

Uh-oh, Mikey thought. She didn't want to spend another day being told how bossy she was. She didn't think she was all that bossy, anyway.

"Yes, we should," Mikey said. "If you don't like meat loaf I'll be just as happy not to share, but that doesn't mean I don't *want* to. Because it *is* good."

"What if it was bad?" Margalo asked.

"Then we should share so I won't have to eat a whole bad one."

They were about to laugh when somebody screamed.

It was Rhonda, backing out of her desk and screaming at the sight of her own lunch.

Rhonda's scream rose up in the air around her, and twisted like red-hot wire.

Goose bumps rose up on Margalo's arm. "Look at that," she said, holding her arm out to show Mikey. "Neat."

Rhonda screamed again, and screamed again.

"What's wrong?" people asked. "Rhonda? Are you all right?" They got out of their desks, and some went to stand by the doors while some crowded around Rhonda's seat. "What's the matter, Rhonda?"

"Stop the noise. Now. Please, stop, so I can see what's going on, Rhonda. Rhonda, are you listening to me?"

Rhonda changed screams, to the sound of a siren, driving away.

"Will you look at that," Louis Caselli said. "Mrs. Chemsky? Look at this."

Rhonda had gotten down to gulping and howling.

"Wow," and "Gross," and "Cool," were the opinions of the boys crowding around Rhonda's desk. Rhonda had gone to cling and sob with Karen. "Horrible," and "Who would do —" were what other people were saying. "Put it *down!*" somebody said.

Louis held a squirrel by its tail. "It's dead," he told anyone who couldn't figure that out from its dangling head.

"For how long?" Sal asked and "Roadkill," Justin

suggested and "Electrocuted," was Noah's opinion, "by overhead wires. Then run over by a few cars. Not very many."

"Maybe it has rabies," Hadrian Klenk said hopefully.

"Why don't you put it back into the bag, if you would, please, Louis?" Mrs. Chemsky asked. "Justin, why don't you hold the bag open so Louis can drop the squirrel in."

So they did, and Mrs. Chemsky took the bag and rolled the top closed. She carried it out into the hallway, to get rid of it somewhere else, they guessed. Maybe the teachers' lounge.

"Where's my lunch?" Rhonda wailed. "Somebody stole my lunch! It's not *fair!*"

Mrs. Chemsky returned, to soothe Rhonda, and to arrange for people to give extra parts of their lunch to Rhonda. "I'm sure," Mrs. Chemsky said, but she didn't finish the sentence. She patted Rhonda's shoulder, and told her there was no need to call her mother at work. "Have something to eat," Mrs. Chemsky said. "Try to calm down. It'll turn up," she promised. She didn't say what *it* was.

Outside, Mikey didn't go right to the soccer game. She wondered whether she shouldn't take a lunch off from soccer, every now and then, sometimes. "How about that squirrel?" Mikey asked.

Margalo grinned. "Would you have guessed

Rhonda was such a good screamer? She's a great screamer."

"No I mean, do you think the squirrel was on purpose?"

"What?" Margalo asked. "The dead squirrel? What do you mean on purpose? Are you asking me if I think the squirrel got itself killed and then just before he died he ran into a brown paper bag, because for some reason he wanted to die in a brown paper bag. Which happened to be near Rhonda's books? Or are you asking if it was Rhonda on purpose? In which case, in my opinion, it probably was. Yes. She's pretty awful."

"I don't like her," Mikey said, "but I'm not sure I think she's much worse than anyone else. Not that everyone else is so great."

"You don't like many people," Margalo observed.

Mikey agreed. "People are pretty much jerks. Do you?"

"Most of them I like OK. Mostly, they're OK. They can't hurt me," Margalo said.

What they were thinking right then was exactly the same thing, if they had known it. They both wanted to forget the way last week had gone out of control.

Neither of them felt like apologizing, either.

By lunchtime Wednesday, everyone had pretty much forgotten about Rhonda's squirrel. That subject had been talked about on Tuesday, until it was talked out. It had been the conversation in all four of the fifth- and sixth-grade classrooms, and then on all of the school buses all the way home.

"Where do you think Rhonda's squirrel came from?"

"I don't think it was personal for you, Rhonda. You don't have anything special about squirrels, do you?"

"How's your squirrel, Rhonda?"

"I think we ought to have given Rhonda's squirrel a decent burial. Not just tossed it into the garbage. What if that squirrel had a home, a wife, and children?"

"Somebody should tell Mrs. Chemsky that we want Rhonda's squirrel back."

On Wednesday, attention had switched over to the soccer game against Riverside, because this year they might not get creamed.

This year, they might even do OK, like, a tie.

Or win, this year they might win. Everybody wanted to win, this year, and everybody was trying not to talk about the game, which was only one week off.

So at Wednesday lunch when Rhonda screamed again, and it was another four-star scream — like a coed in a horror movie, who is about to get her face ripped away, or her throat ripped open, or her heart ripped out, or her arms and legs ripped off, and she has just seen the shadow of the killer —

When Rhonda screamed they were all about as surprised and shocked and excited as they had been the day before.

This time Mrs. Chemsky moved fast. She was the first one there at Rhonda's desk. "Rhonda? Again? Another?" She stood guard at the desk. "The rest of you, just sit down — *down*, Louis — and stay seated. Don't cry, Rhonda. It'll be all right. There, now" — patting Rhonda on her heaving shoulder — "just give it to — I'll take care of whatever —" Mrs. Chemsky said, then "Ackhaoow," she said as she looked into Rhonda's lunch bag. "Oh dear. Oh, you poor child."

"What is it?" everybody wanted to know. "What did she get this time?"

"Another squirrel?"

"Something worse, like, a kitten?"

"A kitten wouldn't fit in a lunch bag, pinhead."

"It would if it was mushed enough, dummy."

"Poor Rhonda. Who do you think is doing this to her?"

That was the question of the day: Who stole Rhonda's lunch and left her a bag of garbage?

Mrs. Chemsky and Rhonda went to Mr. Delaney's office, to talk about that question, and Miss

Carter, who was Mr. Delaney's secretary, gave Mrs. Chemsky's class a study hall.

During Miss Carter's study hall, Margalo and Mikey exchanged notes about the mystery.

There was no mystery to why anyone might hate Rhonda enough to do this, they agreed about that.

— *Its probly a boy,* Mikey wrote.

Margalo didn't correct the errors. — *Why do you say that?*

— *No gril has the gouts to get a roadkill. Ecept me, but I didn't.*

— *Do you wish you had?*

— *I wuldnt mind. What about you?*

— *What about me what?*

They passed the sheet of paper back and forth, writing quickly.

— *Do you wish it was you?* Mikey wrote.

— *If I did, then it would be me. So it's not you?*

— *Louis? Harvey? Sal never werks alon, thats not his MO.*

Margalo answered slowly, as if she was thinking hard about what she was writing. — *Is Hadrian weird enough to do something like this?*

They both turned to look at Hadrian Klenk, by far the scrawniest and shortest person in the class, his hair an inch-high buzz, his shoes plain white sneakers with plain white laces. He belted his khakis tight at the waist.

Margalo grabbed the paper back and crossed out the question she had written, blacking out each word so hard there was almost no point left on her pencil. — *I don't think Hadrian would do anything like this. You don't think he would, do you?*

— *I dont think he nos enuff to now that Rhonda diserves it.*

— *Does she?* Margalo asked. *Why do you think that?*

Mikey turned the paper over to ask, — *Culd we trase the stuff that was in the lunch?*

— *You mean, touch it? Go through somebody's garbage and we don't even know whose?*

— *It's not mutch. Just a bag. Why didn't it leke?*

— *I'd have used a plastic sack.*

— *We culd trase the sack.*

Mikey was really enjoying herself in this note-writing detection conversation. She felt like she was in charge of things again, like, her life.

— *Next time, lets get thier fast and check whats in the bag.*

— *You think there'll be a next time?* Margalo wondered.

— *I don't no. Everwon will be watsching. If it was me, I wuldn't risk it.*

*   *   *

At the start of activities, Mikey showed Margalo a model car her parents had gotten her. "On Saturday. To make me feel better."

"For losing the election?" Margalo asked. "How did they find out? You mean, you told them about it?"

"Of course. I knew they'd want to make it up to me."

"I wouldn't tell. I never did. Not even if I won."

"So you were a president in your old school."

"Sometimes. Weren't you?"

"Lots. How about this?" Mikey asked, handing Margalo a box.

It was a classic, the '56 two-seater T-Bird; a convertible, with a rear-mounted spare tire. It was red. It was exactly the car anybody would want.

"It's great," Margalo said. "It's just — this is a great car, Mikey."

"Yeah, I liked it better than the Corvette. I got it for us to do together."

"Oh," Margalo said. "Wow," she said. "You mean it?" she said.

"No," Mikey said. "I just said it so that when you asked me if I meant it I could say no, and watch your face fall. What do you *think*?"

They set right to work. They only had the hour of

activities. Because the model was metal, there was some initial smoothing down of some edges that needed to be done. Mikey had thought of every-thing, even of bringing two small files. And working at the kind of task they were, it was natural to just talk, about this and that, number 2 versus number 4 pencils, previous schools they'd been in, and what they could talk to their parents about without them going nuts. Then Mikey stopped filing and called across the room, "Louis Caselli?"

"Mee-Shell Elsinger?" he answered.

People pretended not to be listening. Mrs. Chem-sky looked up from her desk work.

"You're the garbage king," Mikey said. "Did you go through Rhonda's garbage?"

"I don't even know where she lives, dumbo," Louis answered.

"Yes, you do, around the corner from me," Ira said.

"Not that garbage," Mikey insisted. She rolled her eyes at Margalo. "The garbage in her lunch bag."

"Why would I do that?" Louis asked. "You're much more likely to go looking through someone's garbage. For a little snack," he smirked.

"I thought you might be playing Encyclopedia Brown," Mikey said. "What happened to the garbage?"

"They took it with them to the office," Louis said. "But I asked Rhonda —"

Mikey smiled an *I-knew-it* smile at Margalo.

"She said coffee grounds, and banana peels, Froot Loops and Cocoa Puffs with milk, toast crusts from white bread. Nothing with an address on."

Having gotten what she wanted, Mikey had nothing more to say to Louis. She seemed to be thinking, so Margalo, who was thinking pretty hard herself, didn't say anything. They filed away at the windshield and the bumpers, and thought away.

"Mee-Shell?" Louis finally asked.

Mikey didn't even look up.

"Why'd you want to know?" Louis asked, after a while. "You want to know if you left something traceable?"

"Are you talking to me?" Mikey inquired.

"Who else? Do you think you've gotten away with it?"

"*I'm* not the kind of person who does things from behind someone's back," Mikey reminded everyone.

The next day, which was Thursday, Rhonda put her lunch bag, with her name written on it in big Magic Marker black letters, on Mrs. Chemsky's desk. "There," she said, with a toss of her long blonde hair. She looked around at the class, daring anyone to try to do something now.

When she was sure everyone was watching, Mrs. Chemsky put the bag into her middle right-hand drawer.

Rhonda flounced over to her seat, and sat down in it. She was the only person Margalo had ever seen who could flounce sitting down.

Margalo grinned at Mikey, and Mikey grinned right back. There was nothing like a real crisis to make a day exciting.

Or at least give it the promise of excitement. Nothing happened on Thursday.

On Friday, flouncing up to put her lunch bag on Mrs. Chemsky's desk again, flouncing back to her seat, Rhonda let them all know how things stood: Her parents were angry, and the teachers were on her side, against whoever it was who was doing this terrible thing to her. All the adults were on Rhonda's side.

And so were her friends. And anyone who wasn't, wasn't her friend. And might even be the person who was doing this. Who was going to get into serious trouble, Rhonda could promise that. Her father was talking about A Lawyer. Her mother didn't think someone with such a disturbed mind ought to be in the regular classroom, with normal people. *So there.*

Everybody kept an eye on Mrs. Chemsky's desk. Nobody wanted to go up to the teacher that morning. Everybody knew that whoever went up to the desk was going to be seriously stared at, and also automatically suspicious.

Nobody could stand to look at Rhonda at all. They felt sorry for her, because somebody was out to get her. They felt bad because they could sort of see how she had asked for it, even if she shouldn't have had to get it. They felt like she was complaining, and letting whoever it was see how upset she was, which were not cool ways to act. They felt like she was blaming all of them for not taking better care of poor little her — and nobody felt like taking any blame because nobody felt like they had done anything.

With one exception, of course.

And that exception took advantage of morning recess to put a brown lunch bag, with Rhonda's name written on it in big Magic Marker letters, under her desk.

Rhonda didn't notice the bag until about halfway through the social studies class on railroads. They were in the middle of Mrs. Chemsky's telling them about the Chinese laborers who laid the railroad tracks. "That's just like they were slaves," Malcolm Johnson remarked and Mrs. Chemsky told him, "African-Americans are not the only exploited people, in the history of America." Noah added, "Actually, it's only WASPs who have never been exploited. Actually, it's only male WASPs, which makes us a real minority —"

And Rhonda gasped. She gasped the kind of gasp that always makes people look, the kind you should never gasp when someone is driving you in a car.

Rhonda gasped in, and then she screamed out, a weak watery scream, like the last spurt out of a mustard dispenser. It was a little and lumpy gasp-and-scream, and it focused the attention of the whole room.

"Ooohoow, *smell,* it's —" Rhonda stood up. Her little scream turned into wailing.

The class waited.

Mrs. Chemsky hesitated, standing before the chalkboard with a piece of chalk in her hand.

Everybody watched Rhonda.

Rhonda reached under her seat. She pulled out the bag, with her name on it. She unrolled the top of the brown paper bag.

The smell — which was a stench, a stink, putrid, rank and foul — flowed up out of the bag like Aladdin's genie coming out of his bottle, and spread out around Rhonda's desk. People grabbed for their noses.

"Get that —!"

"— away from —!"

"What is —?"

"— out of the —"

"— never smelled anything so —"

"— dead fish —"

"— dead fish wrapped in rotten liver —"

By then, Mrs. Chemsky had taken the bag out of Rhonda's hands, sniffed it once, and rolled the top shut again. Rolled up shut the bag only stunk faintly, like somebody was wearing too much perfume, except a perfume that is supposed to drive people away, not make them fall in love with you. Mrs. Chemsky set the bag down on her desk. It waited there, stinking quietly.

"Class," Mrs. Chemsky began.

But Rhonda interrupted her. "Who wants to do this to me? Why would someone put something like that under my desk? With my name on it?"

"— only Limburger cheese," Mrs. Chemsky was telling her class.

"Maybe," Margalo suggested, "someone wants to tell you that you stink."

"I do not," Rhonda said. "Who'd be so mean. To say that to me. Who even thinks that?"

"Me," Margalo said.

Everybody was busy making murmuring sympathetic noises, "Oh no," "Poor you," "I'm sorry," or busy making remarks like "Which came first, the Limburger or the stink?" or busy trying to call the class to order, or busy whimpering and looking around for sympathy, so busy that at first nobody registered what Margalo had said.

Then a little puddle of silence happened.

"Good for you," Mikey whispered, and smiled around at everybody with a *What're-you-going-to-do-about-it?* smile.

The puddle of silence spread out into a circle.

"It's her!" screeched Rhonda. "She's the one!" She stuck her arm straight out, and aimed a finger at Margalo.

Mikey looked at Margalo. Margalo looked uncomfortable, but also sort of smirky.

"You all heard her!" screeched Rhonda. "She can't deny it now!"

"I'm not denying it," Margalo said.

"You're mean! and horrible! and you're in big trouble!"

Margalo sat stiffly with her sweater a bright red and her normally pale cheeks a bright pink, and her brown hair hanging down straight beside her cheeks. She tucked her hair behind her right ear. She tucked her hair behind her left ear.

"Can you explain yourself, Margalo?" Mrs. Chemsky inquired.

"She had no right to talk like that about Mikey."

"I never said anything about Mikey," Rhonda answered.

"Liar," Margalo said. "Big liar."

Tanisha chimed in. "Yes you did. And I thought it was mean, mean and personal."

"I can take care of myself," Mikey butted in. "I didn't care what Rhonda said. She can't hurt me."

"Well, Margalo," Mrs. Chemsky said. Her right hand twisted the wedding ring on her left hand. "I think we had better go see Mr. Delaney about this. Don't you?"

Margalo stood up. She didn't look as if she even knew how much trouble she was in. Or, if she did know, she looked as if maybe she didn't even care.

"I'm coming, too," Rhonda said. "I'm the injured party."

"Sit down, Rhonda," Mrs. Chemsky said.

"That's not fair," Rhonda protested.

"You, too, Miss Elsinger," Mrs. Chemsky said. "You sit down, too. Miss Carter will be here to keep an eye on you," she told her class. "Your assignment is to finish the chapter, reading silently, and then answer in writing the five questions at the end. I apologize for the interruption to your work period. Sit *down*, Miss Elsinger."

"But I should go, too," Mikey said.

"Talk about someone who can't stand not being the center of attention," Louis Caselli said.

Mikey faced off against Louis and bared her teeth, not even pretending it was a smile. Then she turned back to Mrs. Chemsky. This was the more important fight. "I knew. I knew it was Margalo. So I should have to go to Mr. Delaney's office, too. I knew and I didn't try to stop her, and I didn't tell you, so I'm just as bad."

"She is!" Rhonda cried. "She wanted me to be picked on!"

"That," Louis Caselli announced, "is not what's so bad about her. Look, she's going to cry some more," he said, and laughed, while Rhonda wiped furiously at her running nose, and running eyes.

"Silence." Mrs. Chemsky's voice was so low and dangerous that even Rhonda obeyed. "You will remain silent, while you are supervised, and while you are unsupervised. I am not in a mood to be reasonable, with any of you. Is that clear?"

It was perfectly clear. It was absolutely clear. They were almost glad Mrs. Chemsky had gotten angry.

"You two," Mrs. Chemsky pointed, "come with me." She strode out of the room without looking behind her.

She was followed by Mikey first, and then Margalo. Both of the girls wore sneakers, so they didn't make any noise when they walked. Mrs. Chemsky had leather soles, and she tapped.

"You did not know," Margalo said, catching up with Mikey out in the hallway.

What she said sounded like a quarrel but the way she was walking beside Mikey was friendly. Mikey decided to take the friendly.

"Did, too. I guessed when I thought since it wasn't me, who it might be. Which was you," Mikey said. "Then I saw the paper bag in your book bag, yest —"

"You went looking in my book bag?"

"How else was I going to find out?" Mikey asked, but if she was honest she'd have to say she knew at the time it was wrong. She didn't do it *because* it was wrong, but she didn't *not* do it for that reason. "But you didn't *tell* me."

"I was going to," Margalo said.

Mrs. Chemsky parked them on the bench outside Mr. Delaney's door. She asked Miss Carter to go supervise the class, and whispered briefly in the young woman's ear. "Ohhh, ahhh," Miss Carter said, and gave them a look before she scurried off. Mrs. Chemsky told Margalo and Mikey to wait there, please. She knocked on the door to the office, and went in, closing it behind her.

Mikey and Margalo sat side by side. Neither one of them said anything. There didn't seem to be anything to say. Then, "What were you going to use next?" Mikey asked. "If you hadn't told."

"I wasn't sure," Margalo said. "I might have been running out of ideas, or maybe some of the chips and newspapers from my little brothers' gerbil cage. They have to clean it out, every Thursday. What I really wanted to do was have one of the bags delivered by one of those singing messengers. I've seen them on TV, and they're in the yellow pages." Margalo swung her feet and smiled to herself. "You know? He could have come into the classroom, and he'd sing the nobody likes me song. You know?" She hummed the tune and Mikey hummed along. "Only I'd have him sing 'Nobody likes *you*, everybody hates *you*,'" Margalo sang. They sang the last lines together. "Go out to the garden and eat worms," and added the same extra last words, together: "Rhonda Ransom."

Mikey was laughing.

"But it's too expensive."

"Did you call up and get a price? Did you really do that?"

"It's too late now, anyway. Oh well, maybe next time," Margalo laughed, too. "I don't think he'll let you stay. It isn't as if you did it, or asked me to, or anything."

"They can't *make* me leave. Unless they carry me out."

Margalo felt full of feelings, all kinds of feelings. She told Mikey, "You know, you should know, I should tell you. Since. I mean. You think I have a crush on Lee, don't you?"

Mikey was feeling good about herself, right then. She really liked herself. "It's plain as the nose on your face," she said.

"But I don't," Margalo said. She looked down at her hands, which held onto one another in her lap. "It's Ira."

"Ira? Ira Pliotes? Ira who you voted for? You have a crush on Ira?"

Margalo nodded, once, twice, three, four times.

"Oh," Mikey said. "Because he's nice," Mikey explained it. "And sort of cute, too. Does he like you back?"

Margalo had no idea, but she pretty much doubted it. She thought probably he liked Ronnie.

"Maybe he likes you next," Mikey said.

From behind the office door, they could hear the two voices talking, one man's and one woman's.

"I don't have anyone I like," Mikey said.

"That doesn't matter," Margalo said. She hoped she wouldn't regret telling Mikey. She didn't think she would, but you couldn't be sure.

"My father used to do coke," Mikey said. "In college," she said. "And after, too." She'd never told anyone that, ever.

It took Margalo a minute to figure it out. "Not Coke the drink," she said at last. She didn't dare to ask the question that was in her mind.

Mikey shook her head. "He's not a *dealer*, he's not

a criminal, he never got caught. But — he'd act — funny. It was scary."

"I can imagine," Margalo said, although she couldn't. Sometimes, when her stepfathers got angry, she'd be scared, especially if she was afraid they'd find out something she'd disobeyed about. But that was just normal stuff, for families, just kids trying to get away with stuff and parents trying to catch them. Coke was drugs. Coke was scary in a whole lot of ways Margalo knew she'd never had to deal with. "I can't imagine," Margalo said.

"He still does," Mikey said, her hands holding onto her knees. She was smiling but she didn't have any idea what kind of smile it was. "He still is. Sometimes."

"Oh," Margalo said, again. Then she asked, "What are you going to do?"

"What *can* I do?" Mikey asked. "Nothing. Big, fat nothing. He's not a bad guy."

"I didn't mean —"

The office door opened, and Mrs. Chemsky told them to come in, please.

Mikey let Margalo go first, because Margalo had done the real work of getting into this much trouble.

Mr. Delaney was sitting behind his desk. He wore a light-gray plaid jacket, with a green V-neck sweater, and his shirt collar open.

Both Margalo and Mikey noticed it right away: It was different when the person you were in trouble with was the principal, and a man. Two empty chairs waited in front of his desk. Mrs. Chemsky waited at the door.

Mrs. Chemsky said, "Margalo? I've told Mr. Delaney what I saw going on. You should tell him the story as you saw it."

"Yes, Mrs. Chemsky."

"Miss Elsinger?" Mikey turned to look at the teacher. "I'm not convinced you have earned the right to be here."

"I have," Mikey said. "I did," she said. "Honest," she said.

"Well," Mrs. Chemsky said.

Mikey and Margalo both decided that she didn't want to leave them there alone with the principal. When they talked this over later, they agreed that their teacher seemed reluctant to leave them.

Mr. Delaney told Mrs. Chemsky, "I'll send them back to the classroom when I'm through with them. I don't think it'll be long."

"Thank you," Mrs. Chemsky said, and pulled the door closed after her. This left just the three of them in the room.

"Well," Mr. Delaney said, from behind his desk.

He was broad in the shoulders, and deep voiced. He was clean shaven, and his hair was trimmed short. He used to be a coach, before he became an administrator. He looked them straight in the eye, first Mikey, straight in the eye, then Margalo.

"I'm the one who did it," Margalo said and she told him why Rhonda had it coming.

"She had a dead squirrel coming?" Mr. Delaney asked.

Margalo explained: "Dogs are much too big, and cats — well, a cat is still pretty big for a brown lunch bag. And there's something sad about dogs and cats, because they're pets, or they used to be before they got run over. I'd have liked a bird but I didn't find any. Or a chipmunk, maybe. But all I could find was a couple of squirrels, so I picked the best one."

"I see." He tapped his pencil on the desk. "What made it the best?"

"It was the most squished," Margalo explained. "To get even," she explained.

"Ditto the garbage? Ditto the Limburger?"

"I had to buy the cheese," Margalo said. "But it was past its sale date, so I got it cheap."

"I'm glad to hear that," Mr. Delaney said.

Margalo smiled. "You're being sarcastic," she said. "But I'm not sorry. Rhonda does stink. What she did stinks."

"So did what you did," Mr. Delaney said. "Think about it."

"Oh," Margalo said.

"And do you feel any better now?"

"Yes," Margalo said. "I do."

"Even knowing how much trouble you've gotten yourself into?"

Mr. Delaney was losing patience.

"I'm in the same trouble," Mikey butted in.

"Ah, yes. And can you go through it again for me, Mikey? Why you are supposed to be equally guilty?"

Mikey went through it again. "Because I knew. I knew all along." Margalo turned to object, but Mikey kept talking. "So because I knew and didn't try to stop her, I'm an accomplice, aren't I? That's almost as bad, and I was the cause, too."

They talked this over, too, later. "You *didn't* know from the first, did you really?" Margalo asked. "I know you didn't, you said so. You did say so, didn't you?"

"What does that matter?" Mikey asked. "Mr. Delaney knew what I meant."

Mr. Delaney had asked Mikey, "Let me be sure I've got this straight. Did you *hire* your friend to perform acts of harassment?"

"Of course not. I'd have done it myself, if I'd thought of it."

"Given that, in what way are you responsible? Can you make it clearer to me?" Mr. Delaney put down his pencil and leaned his elbows on his desk; he laced his fingers together. He looked like some

TV judge, about to say something wise. He looked so much like a TV judge that they both knew how sarcastic he was being.

"Accessory after the fact," Mikey finally found the phrase. "Isn't that what I am? If Margalo had been stealing money from Mrs. Chemsky's purse, and I knew it, and I didn't report her, wouldn't you think I was just as bad as she was? Wouldn't you think I was just as guilty? For not turning her in," she explained.

"Even though you didn't take an active part in the misdeeds."

"I was actively choosing not to do anything to stop her."

"I don't see that that is the same as being actively involved," Mr. Delaney said.

"I bet if you asked Rhonda, she wouldn't say that. Or would her father," Mikey maintained, and that won the argument for her. It was the parents that did it, every time.

Mr. Delaney leaned back, and drummed his right hand fingers on the top of his desk. "All right," he said. "All right. This is your punishment. First, by the end of next week, you are each going to have to have presented to Rhonda a letter of apology. Mrs. Chemsky will read them before you present them."

"But that would be lying, if I apologized," Margalo said.

Mr. Delaney continued, as if Margalo hadn't spoken. "Rhonda will also be writing a note of apology, to you, Mikey. My advice to you two is this: If lying troubles you so deeply," he said, with a wide-eyed sarcasm, "perhaps you might put your heads together to find a way to both accept responsibility and tell the truth."

Margalo looked at Mikey. Mikey looked at Margalo. Later, when they talked, they realized that they had both been having exactly the same thought: They were really glad to be in this together.

"Moreover," Mr. Delaney said, "you will both be on detention, all next week. Every day. After school. Mrs. Chemsky will be there to assign you various tasks to benefit the school environment. This will, we hope, remind you that school is a place we all inhabit together. In order for our habitat to be a good place for all of us, all of us have to follow certain rules of conduct. Do you understand what I am trying to say to you?"

"Yes, Mr. Delaney," they said.

"Finally," he told them, "I will be phoning your parents. To apprise them of what has gone on, and how the school is responding to that." He let those words settle slowly onto the floor of the room before he dismissed Margalo and Mikey. "That is all. You may return to your classroom now. A note of apology, remember, and then five days of detention.

You've gotten off lightly," he warned them. "From me," he added ominously.

For the rest of the day they got exactly the same treatment from the class, too — embarrassed silence, angry staring, uncomfortable looking away. Everybody in the class seemed to agree, even Rhonda, even Louis, even Tanisha and Ronnie. Everybody seemed to agree that nobody wanted to be in the same room as Mikey and Margalo, or on the same playground, or in the same line for buses. Everybody didn't have anything to say to them.

So they sang their song, whenever either one of them started feeling seriously bad. One of them would start it and the other would join in. "Nobody likes me," Margalo might sing, softly, and Mikey would grin back at her. "Everybody hates me, Going to the garden to eat worms." They kept changing the next lines, to get them to their worst possibilities: big fat gooey worms, long thin slimy worms, bloated worms, swollen, oozy, squirmy.

Squirmy, they agreed, was just about as bad as it got. Singing together, trying to top one another for badness, cheered them up enough to get them through the rest of the day.

8

Out in the Garden Eating Worms

Mikey and Margalo were so glad to see each other on Monday morning, each one wanted to apologize for never calling up over the weekend, even though they never had telephoned before. Neither one knew the other's number.

Neither one said how she was feeling, either.

But.

But Mikey smiled at Margalo's pale, oval face, as if Margalo was a puppy in a box, and Mikey had always wanted a puppy, and at last she was going to get to pick one out, and she chose this one. And Margalo was smiling at Mikey as if she had been swimming for hours from a capsized canoe, and there was the shore, she could see it, and now she knew she'd make it.

"Hey," Margalo said.

"I just realized — you could have been sick today," Mikey said.

"I thought about it," Margalo said. "Didn't you? But, I thought you wouldn't, so I didn't, either. Were your parents bad?"

"The usual stuff about permanent record, but otherwise no. As long as I don't get picked up by the police, I guess they'll leave me alone."

"Lucky," Margalo said.

They walked on.

Slowly.

The longest way to the classroom was to go up the broad sidewalk, then through the double doors of the front entry, past Mr. Delaney's office and across the big central auditorium space, and then right, to Mrs. Chemsky's classroom. Mikey and Margalo started slowly up the main sidewalk, taking the longest way.

Finally, Margalo demanded, "Aren't you going to ask me about mine? Gees, Mikey. As if you were the only one who has parents to get on her case." For some reason, she could feel herself getting emotional, and quarrelsome. It was going to be bad at school today, and she wished it would just start.

"Are you saying I'm selfish?" Mikey demanded. She wouldn't mind a good fight, right now. If she started out angry, then she'd get through the day all right. She knew that about herself.

"No. I'm saying how wonderful you are."

"Oh."

"The way you're so interested in what happens to me," Margalo said.

But what did Margalo mean, saying that, when she'd just been complaining that Mikey acted like the only one with parents?

"And making sure I didn't get into serious trouble at home, or anything, being so sympathetic," Margalo said.

Mikey got it now. This was sarcasm.

"Because you're such a good friend," Margalo said.

Margalo had a right to be sarcastic. Mikey hadn't even wondered.

"What do you think I meant, stupid?" Margalo demanded, turning away because her eyes were filled with water that she blinked furiously at.

"I'm sorry," Mikey said. "Really, really I am. It was selfish, you're right." Now Mikey felt both bad, for having been unintentionally selfish, and good, for having apologized right away. "What *did* happen?" Of course she wanted to know. "Was it awful?"

"They grounded me for the weekend, not that that made any difference. It's not as if I had any plans. I was under house arrest, you know? I couldn't go outside, the usual —"

"I'm glad you told me when I was being selfish," Mikey interrupted. "I don't — well not with you, anyway, I don't want to be; otherwise I don't mind."

And there was Margalo laughing now. Laughing at her. "What's so funny?" Mikey demanded.

"Nothing," Margalo laughed. "You." Margalo didn't know what she was doing, laughing. "We aren't going to be very popular today," Margalo said.

They were going up the broad front steps.

"You better believe it," Mikey agreed.

"Detention will be the easy part."

"You're a real Little Miss Sunshine today." Then Mikey grinned, a Gingerbread Man grin, *Catch-me-if-you-can.* "We can get through this," she said.

"I hope so. Besides, what can they do to us?"

They went through the doorway, into the building.

"Other then make fun of us, or ostracize us, or call us names, or try to beat us up? Steal our homework papers? Stomp on our lunch boxes? Accuse us of taking their money or pencils? of cheating off them? Make up stories about us to tell the teachers? Hate us for the rest of the year? for the rest of our lives?" Mikey pretended to be thinking hard. "Other than making our lives as miserable as possible for as long as possible, they can't do anything much. Why do you ask?"

Margalo was laughing again, a belling laugh out of her stomach. "Well, that's all right then," she said.

If Margalo thought it was all right, then who was Mikey to argue with her? If Margalo could manage, so could Mikey. Mikey led Margalo across the auditorium and through the fire door. They walked together down the hall.

About half of the class had already arrived in the room. Everybody got quiet when Margalo and Mikey entered, then everybody talked too loudly. Nobody looked at or spoke to either Mikey or Margalo.

It didn't exactly feel as if everybody was staring at their backs, as they hung up their sweaters and took paper, pencils, notebooks, and reading texts out of their bookbags. It didn't exactly feel like everybody was voodooing bad luck on them. It just felt like they were different from everybody.

At odds with the rest of the class, and the rest of the school, too.

But, together. Different together. At odds together.

Mikey looked at Margalo and smiled her new wrinkledy *Eat-prunes* smile. Margalo crossed her eyes, hung her tongue out, tilted her head to one side. They turned around together. To see what they were up against. Spinning around like Butch Cassidy and the Sundance Kid, ready for trouble.

Mrs. Chemsky sat at her desk, adding columns of numbers in her attendance book. Ronnie and some friends were talking away, across the room, looking at Derrie's ears, where gold studs had appeared over the weekend. Hadrian sat alone, reading a computer magazine, or maybe it was a miniatures magazine, or an issue of *Money*; you never could tell which of Hadrian's obsessions he was going to bring a magazine about when he came to school. The boys were mostly outside, but just then the bell rang, and the volume of noise in the room rose.

Nobody said anything.

Nobody didn't say anything, either.

Tanisha walked by their desks, on her way to her own, and tapped with her fingers on Mikey's desk, going by. "Hey," Tanisha said, and went on. Mrs. Chemsky raised her head and looked at Mikey, and at Margalo. She raised her eyebrows and kept them up for a while, to tell them *what*, Mikey had no idea.

It was Louis who broke the ice. Louis parked himself in front of Margalo. "You didn't even get suspended," he said. "Because you're a girl," he said. "Boy, are you going to get it."

"Get what?" Margalo asked. Why was Louis so

246

angry at her now? Did he think she was scared of him?

"What is it, do you have a crush on Rhonda?" Mikey asked. "Is she your new girlfriend and you're being all manly and protective?"

"Stuff it," Louis said.

Mikey stood up, clear of her seat, facing him face on.

"I'm not afraid of you," Louis said. "Or you, either, sneakface," he said to Margalo. "You and your baby punishments."

Mikey's hands were balled into fists, but she was keeping her temper. Louis also was trying to keep his temper and Mrs. Chemsky was just watching them, watching them closely. It was obvious that what both Louis and Mikey wished was that they could have a good punchout.

"Oh well," Mikey said. She smiled an evil smile, but she held out her hand. While Louis was studying her hand and deciding if she meant him to shake it, and if he *had* to shake it, and how he could refuse to shake it and show how he hated her — Mikey kicked him in the shin. She kicked him hard and sharp, as hard and sharp as she could with sneakers.

Mrs. Chemsky put her pencil down. "Miss —"

"Oh, ow!" Mikey cried.

It *hurt* to kick him. It was like she'd kicked a stone, or a brick wall. It really hurt. Mikey hopped on her left leg, clutching her right foot in her hands. It hurt too much to even worry about people seeing that it hurt.

Mrs. Chemsky watched.

"Ha," Louis Caselli said. He turned and strutted back to his desk. He sat down, smirking around at everyone. As if he had an itch that needed scratching, he reached down and rubbed at his shin.

"Everyone," Mrs. Chemsky said. "Sit —"

And Rhonda stood in the doorway. She let everyone notice her and get quiet before she entered the room. *She* made it clear. *She* wasn't about to even *look* at Mikey, or at Margalo. *She* wasn't going to say a single word to them. Ever. She flounced across to her cubby. She tossed her long, blonde hair. She took her books to her seat. When she got there, and sat, she turned around to talk to Ann Tarwell, behind her, and then the other way to whisper to Lindsey Westerburg. The whispers were loud and angry.

The second bell rang.

"Keith Adams," Mrs. Chemsky called and "Here," Keith answered quickly. "Karen Blackaway."

At the end of attendance, Mrs. Chemsky announced to her class what Mr. Delaney and she had decided the disciplinary measures to be taken would be, for all three of the girls involved. She announced that it was time for this class to settle down. "And I do mean settle down," Mrs. Chemsky added. "I am about at the end of my year's supply of patience. Yes, Rhonda?"

"You're not cross with *me*, are you?" Rhonda asked. "You can't be, because I'm the injured party. And my father," she announced to everyone, "is talking about suing."

Everybody had already been nervously quiet, hoping things would blow over, and blow back to only normal uproar and upset. Everybody understood that Mrs. Chemsky had just given them fair warning. But now the silence thickened, like setting Jell-O. It was one thing for kids to have quarrels, but when the grown-ups — especially parents — got into it, then all that kids could do was keep their heads down. Kids just threw punches. Parents lobbed bombs.

"I'd like to see him try suing me," Mikey said. She didn't even think about raising her hand.

"Not you, you're just a follower," Rhonda announced. "Her."

She pointed at Margalo.

"She's the Bad Seed," Rhonda announced, her finger still raised and pointing.

Margalo had to admit, this did scare her. Not that she wanted to deny what she had done; it was her fault, and had been her own choice. Not that she minded being called a bad seed, or even being one. But being sued, your stepfather being sued, or your mother — who didn't have a job or income of her own — when you didn't really have a father to stand up for you. And your mother spent her life getting married, and divorced, and having new babies.

"*My* father said," Mikey announced, and turned around to stare right into Rhonda's face, as if there were just the two of them in the room. "*My* father said," Mikey repeated, "that he wouldn't be surprised if you tried something like this. *He's* looking forward to it. He has all the company lawyers to work for us."

Rhonda tossed her blonde head, and humphed. "That's what you say. But we all know what a liar you are. You'd better remember this, though: I'm the offended party."

"Well," Mrs. Chemsky said then. "Well, you know, I wonder," she said, as she walked around to stand in front of her desk. "I wonder, for example, what I myself might testify, if someone asked me to give evidence about what happened. If I told the whole truth and nothing but the truth. I wonder if I'm the only person in the room who remembers pretty exactly what Rhonda said about Miss Elsinger, during the election speeches, which is when all of this started. Let me see what the numbers are: Raise your hand if you can remember what Rhonda said that made Margalo so angry."

Twenty-six hands flew up. Mikey's stayed down, because she couldn't remember and didn't want to. Hadrian's stayed down, as did Rhonda's, Salvatore's, and Noah's.

Rhonda looked nervously around.

"You are such a jerk, Rhonda," Louis Caselli said, as he lowered his hand. "Sorry," he said, when he caught Mrs. Chemsky's eye. Her eye stayed on him until he said, "Sorry, Rhonda."

Three tears rolled out of Rhonda's eyes. Two went down the left cheek, one down the right.

"I agree that the events of last week must have offended you," Mrs. Chemsky said to Rhonda in a perfectly ordinary voice. "But I think I must ask you to understand how you, in your turn, were offensive. Now class, the first spelling word today will be *litigious*."

She wrote it out on the board. Then she wrote, *contentious*. Then Mrs. Chemsky said, out of nowhere and to nobody, "No."

The class looked up.

Mrs. Chemsky announced, "If a teacher isn't grown-up enough to admit she wants to change her mind, how can she expect her students to be able to? I'd like to start the list over again. Ready?" She erased the two words. "This week, we will study the negative prefixes. The first word is *impossible*," she said, "as in not possible."

Mrs. Chemsky looked out the window while they wrote. When they finished writing, the class also looked out the windows, to see what was out there that made their teacher look that way, as if the fire drill bell was ringing in the middle of a major test.

What was out there was a low, dark gray sky that might rain, any minute. Mrs. Chemsky turned to smile at her class. None of them made the mistake of thinking their teacher was happy.

"*Innocent.*" Mrs. Chemsky wrote it on the board. "Can anyone explain to me in what way the word *innocent* is a negative?"

Every single person in the room was hoping that the class wouldn't be kept in for recess, not today.

"Yes, Hadrian?"

Mikey and Margalo overheard what people said about them. "Stuck-up," seemed to be the most frequently whispered words but "bad influence" got mentioned several times, also "two-faced," "bossy," "weird," "smug."

"Not the sharpest pencils out of the box," was Margalo's favorite, since she was sure that wasn't true. Mikey preferred the term "sociopaths." You had to take a sociopath seriously. She convinced herself she hadn't heard the response someone she couldn't see had made to that bit of name-calling, "sociopathic, don't you mean? Socially pathetic, they both are."

When Rhonda was called up to talk with the teacher, at the start of morning recess, which rain kept them inside for, she squeezed between Mikey's desk and Margalo's desk, so they could hear her say, "Now you're in for it."

What the boys were saying was louder, to be sure it was overheard. "Think they can get away with anything. Just because they're stupid girls. Think they're so smart," was the boys' complaint. "Think they can win."

It was like the first day of school, only worse. On the first day of school you knew there was no reason why you couldn't fit in, and you also knew that after not very much time had passed, you would have gotten used to it, and it would have gotten used to you.

It's worse to be disliked by people you know. It's worse to feel out of place where the place is familiar.

Mikey and Margalo shared snacks, and ignored the rest of the room. They traded Oreos for a square of marble cake, with chocolate frosting. "I think it's you," Mikey said to Margalo.

"Of course it is. I did it. If you want to back out —" Margalo didn't finish that sentence.

"Don't be a jerk. I meant, I think it's you Louis has a crush on."

"Oh." Margalo grinned. "Too bad for him if he does. But do you really think so? I'd be surprised. I mean, really surprised. Because I never thought so, and I usually catch on to crushes pretty quickly. I have good radar," she said.

"Not stuck-up at all, are you?" Mikey asked.

"No," Margalo said. "Because it's true, I do know how to figure people out."

"Like how I'm not supposed to say I'm the best soccer player."

"It's like there's some rule about saying nice things about yourself. Even if they're just the truth. Even thinking nice things. How you're not allowed to. It's stupid," Margalo said.

"Besides, it's not probable that everyone does think that," Mikey said.

"Think you're the best at soccer?" Margalo asked.

"No. Think we're stuck-up. That we're so bossy, all that stuff. Two-faced, weird." Mikey had to admit, she didn't care what anyone thought, or said.

"But you know," Margalo answered, "in a way we are. Stuck-up, because that means we don't pretend we don't think we're good at things. And we do make trouble — you know that. And we like making trouble too, or at least I do, and getting in trouble. I do. Don't you?"

"It still doesn't make sense that *everyone* thinks the same about us," Mikey said, sticking to her point. "Everyone almost never agrees about anything, in this class."

"Who cares?" Margalo asked. "Who cares anyway? It's no good to care about what people think when you can't do anything about it anyway."

Ronnie came over to where they sat. She looked down at them. "What you did was mean, Margalo," she said. "It was really mean."

Margalo looked right back at Ronnie and said, "I meant it to be."

"Don't you care if you're in trouble with everybody?"

"Why should I?" Margalo answered, not answering.

"I don't blame you," Ronnie said. "For doing it. I want to say that, too. Or you either, Mikey, I don't blame you, either."

Margalo glared at Mikey, to keep her quiet. Mikey kept quiet but she smiled her *I-told-you-so* smile and she made sure Margalo saw her smiling it.

Mrs. Chemsky had no difficulty getting people settled down to work that day, even when recess was just over.

With the morning recess behind them, lunch, and lunch recess weren't as bad as Mikey had expected. Despite what she'd so confidently said to Margalo, she really hadn't expected anyone to talk to them, so she was surprised that in fact a few people seemed to be on her side. And Margalo's. For a while during the long lunch recess, Tanisha changed desks with Annaliese, and made a small circle with Mikey and Margalo, who were pretending to play chess, pretending that they were interested in learning how a game of chess went.

"It'll all blow over," Tanisha said. "You'll see, by tomorrow or the day after, it'll be blown on away. But you two," she said, just shaking her head at them. "You make my sun to shine, what you get up to, you two. I wouldn't worry about the rest of them. By next week they'll have forgotten all about it. Mostly, anyway. You know," Tanisha said, talking on among the other conversations that washed around the room like waves onto a beach, "it's weird the way what's the right thing to say or do keeps changing. For example," she said, picking up a black pawn Margalo had won from Mikey, and turning it in her long fingers, "my great-grandparents — my mom's grandparents, and my pop's — they were supposed to call themselves Coloreds. To be po-lite and proper, that was the name, when they were young and learning manners. Then my grandparents, it was Negros, and my parents rebelled and said Blacks, black is beautiful. Nowadays if I don't call us African-Americans I'm dissing us, and myself, too. A girl can have trouble keeping up with the changes," Tanisha laughed, "and knowing what's the po-lite thing to call."

But most people didn't say anything to Mikey or to Margalo. They wouldn't look at Margalo. They wouldn't answer any of the questions Mikey asked to find out if someone would answer a question or be struck temporarily totally deaf. "Derrie? What was the seventh spelling word?" "Lynnie? What do you call that color your socks are?" On the other hand, nobody picked any fights. "They're waiting to see how everybody else acts," Mikey told Tanisha and Margalo.

"Go-alongs," Tanisha said.

"Wimps, and whiners, and widget-warmers," Mikey said.

Both Tanisha and Margalo protested. "Widget-warmers?"

Mikey grinned, a *Gotcha* grin. Ira came to stand in front of the three desks where they sat. "I don't think people should be calling you names," Ira said, loud and clear even though a lot of the class was listening.

Margalo wasn't surprised that Ira was brave enough to stand up and say what he thought in front of everyone. She'd never had a crush on somebody not worth having a crush on.

But she was too shy to say even "Thank you."

She could have kicked herself.

Ira had something else to say. "I don't think what you did was very nice, but I can see why you wanted to do it."

In a fit of shyness, Margalo couldn't think of anything to say. But Mikey could. "That's fair," she said. She thought it was pretty nice of Ira to come and make a show of not ignoring them; sort of prissy, but pretty nice. "Margalo agrees," she said.

Ira nodded and moved away, going back to his own seat, his ears reddened at the edges.

"They're like Dumbo's ears," Mikey whispered, teasing.

"Shhhh — please," Margalo whispered.

"When he's flying. Have you ever seen *Dumbo*?" Mikey loved teasing. It meant you had the upper hand. She hated being teased, but that was different.

"What if he hears?"

Margalo was right and she looked really uncomfortable. Mikey shut herself up.

Just about at the end of noon recess, when Tanisha had left Annaliese's desk empty, it was Hadrian Klenk who approached them. He blinked, as if he wore glasses, but he didn't wear glasses. He looked like a little kid, maybe a third-grader, and Margalo had an inspiration. "Hadrian, did you skip?" she asked.

Hadrian blinked, and nodded.

"What grade?" Margalo asked. If the reason he looked and acted so young was because he *was* so young, that made sense.

"Kindergarten."

"So you must have been a big brain right from the first," Mikey joked.

Hadrian didn't look at Mikey. He looked at the toes of his sneakers. He nodded his head, and studied his sneakers, and said, "Second, too."

"Wow," Mikey said. "You're a serious brain."

"I'm sorry," Hadrian said.

"It's OK," Margalo said. "It doesn't matter."

Then there was a long, uncomfortable silence. Hadrian wasn't saying anything. It was as if he had discovered the secret of life in the white rubber toes of his sneakers. He couldn't take his eyes off them.

"So, what do you want?" Mikey asked, after she had waited as long as she could. Hadrian mumbled something. "What?" Mikey asked, loudly.

"People are mean," Hadrian mumbled more clearly. He looked so embarrassed, Margalo just wanted to send him home to his mother, or at least back across the room to his desk and his magazines.

Mikey joked again, "There's a hot news item."

And Hadrian Klenk actually smiled, and looked — just a brief glance — right at Mikey, then — quickly, as if his eyes were scurrying for cover — back to his toes. "You're — I think you're — fine. You too, Margalo. No matter what anyone says. They just — never like anyone different. Because — But it's just —" He looked up again, as if pleading with Mikey, "Because they're afraid."

"Afraid of what?" Mikey asked.

"That they're dweebs and losers," Hadrian explained, earnest.

"They are," Mikey said.

"And that they'll turn out to be — wrong, about everything," Hadrian said.

"They are," Mikey said.

"Not always," Hadrian argued. "Things aren't that — easy. But I'm sorry about — you. And you too, Margalo. It's OK for me, I don't mind — what people think. But they shouldn't be so horrible about you. And you too, Margalo."

"Thank you," Margalo said.

"They'll be the ones who are sorry," Mikey predicted with malicious confidence. "You wait and see."

"I know." Hadrian answered as if he thought

Mikey was just an ordinary person, saying something ordinary.

"Anyway," Hadrian said. He blinked. He scratched at his left ear. "I'm sorry. I didn't — mean to bother — " and before Margalo or Mikey could say anything, Hadrian Klenk was running away from them. Actually running, practically, as if they were somebody wanting to catch him and beat him up.

He looked like he'd always be a person who was easy to beat up, with his pants belted high at the waist. "Do you think he's right?" Margalo asked Mikey.

"About what?"

"About being someone important."

"Absolutely," Mikey said.

"It's a reasonable guess. I can see Hadrian, some mad rocket scientist blowing up the world, or maybe figuring out how to go faster than the speed of light, or cure AIDS, or doing something with inventions, like, microchips, like Microsoft. Do you know about Microsoft? Those guys were weird in school, I bet."

"So being weird means you're something special?" Margalo asked.

"So let's get weird," Mikey said. "You want to? Halloween is coming up, what are you going to be for Halloween? Do you want to have a weird contest?"

"How can there be a contest for just the two of us?" Margalo asked.

"I don't see anybody else wanting to come and play with us, do you? Even Hadrian —"

"I think he has a crush on you," Margalo said.

"Not if he knows what's good for him," Mikey said. "What about, we could be candy machines, and — listen — we could go to houses, and then we could get kids to put money into our slots and we'd give them candy in exchange. That way, we'd make money."

"Or if — if we had costumes we could exchange," Margalo said eagerly. "We could go to a house, and get our stuff, then go behind a tree — like Superman — and change costumes, then go right back again. So we'd get twice as much at each house. Or even," her mind was racing now, "we could start out with ghost sheets over our interchangeable candy machine costumes, and get three shots at each house."

"But what about our contest?" Mikey wanted to know.

"This would be better than a contest. Or we could be Sonny and Cher, and I could be Cher, and I could wear a wig, we could make it out of a mop, dyed black. We could sing," Margalo suggested. "We'd really stink," she promised.

"Chocolate and Vanilla?" Mikey suggested, getting into it now. "I'd have to be Chocolate because my hair is darker."

"Your hair isn't darker. It's greener."

"OK, Peas and Carrots. You could be Carrots. A carrot stick."

And the bell rang. And lunch recess was behind them. And they were back in the relative safety of Mrs. Chemsky's classroom, where Mrs. Chemsky made all the rules and enforced them strictly.

That left only detention to get through.

No, that left only the seven-minute space of time between final bell and bus bell to get through, and then detention.

Most of the day was behind them.

9

Worms À La Mode

When all the other students had left, for cars and buses, for dance class and a soccer strategy meeting, the classroom felt empty. It also felt bigger. The quiet had echoes, like sound shadows.

Margalo and Mikey fiddled around at their cubbies, with their backs to that part of the room where Mrs. Chemsky waited. Mikey pretended to be listening to what Margalo was pretending to be talking about.

Some TV show.

"Margalo?" Mrs. Chemsky said. "Girls?"

They turned around, as if she had caught them doing something forbidden.

In fact, both of them felt guilty. Punishment was the guiltiest-feeling time. Doing the deed was usually satisfying, and confessing was a relief from the tension of worrying if you'd be caught. When you were doing, or confessing to, the deed, it was easy to feel innocent.

But now, facing Mrs. Chemsky, it was harder to remember that they didn't deserve to be punished.

"Come up here, please, girls," Mrs. Chemsky said. She was in front of her big wooden desk, leaning back on it. Her expression didn't give anything away, and her arms were folded in front of her. She was dressed as usual for teaching, trousers, a colored blouse, a long cardigan, flat-heeled shoes, stockings, her hair neat.

"Sit down, please," Mrs. Chemsky said, and they sat down, Mikey in Louis Caselli's desk, Margalo in Salvatore's. These front row desks had the cleanest tops in the classroom; there was nothing interesting to read on them.

Mikey and Margalo looked at one another.

They looked up at the teacher.

"I have given serious thought to you," the teacher said. "A great deal of serious thought, to both of you." They nodded agreement with this statement, and waited. "Do you realize that not only are your initials the same —"

They nodded.

"But also they form a word that is a personal pronoun. The first person, singular, object form. We will come to objects in grammar, so suffice it for now to point out that objects are the centers of attention, in grammar. Or," and Mrs. Chemsky was away on one of those teacher rambles, which seemed to amuse teachers so much, "actually, one of two centers of attention in a sentence. The subject being the other. Curiously," Mrs. Chemsky continued, probably mistaking their unwavering attention as interest, unless she really didn't care if they were interested or not, "little children use that form of the first person singular as either the subject or object in their speech. *Me want*," she gave an example. "*Give me*. Or, rather, *gimme*," she said, finishing her thought up neatly.

They didn't know whether this was the right time to nod, or not. Mikey nodded, and Margalo didn't. Then Margalo, seeing Mikey, started to nod away, while Mikey, noticing that Margalo hadn't, stopped.

"Yes," Mrs. Chemsky said. "But I don't think you've realized yet — and it must be said that we haven't yet done how the abbreviations for the names of the states are often formed —" She hesitated.

Mo, Margalo thought. But that's Missouri, and it's one of the exceptions to the rule of how to form abbreviations for states, but there are as many exceptions as there are states that follow the rules. At least she thought there were.

My, Mikey thought, and smiled with satisfaction.

My, Margalo thought, and grinned, too. That was just like Mikey, to have My and ME initials.

"MO is what criminals have," Mikey said. Margalo said she knew that already, but Mikey was too pleased with her own idea to pay any attention to what Margalo already knew. "It's on cop shows. The MO tells you who the criminal is, because criminals tend to repeat their MOs."

"Mode of Operation is a near enough translation of the Latin," Mrs. Chemsky said, and still added, "*Modus Operandi.*"

Or Me *again,* Mikey thought; *from Michelle. Her initials could be* Me *or* My *or* ME. *That was pretty all right with her.*

Margalo was having a happy thought: *I am something of an operator. I do have an MO, and it works, too, most of the time.*

"So when I was thinking about you two girls," Mrs. Chemsky said, "I reached the conclusion that in the case of Miss Elsinger, I have made an error. A wrong decision. I chose to follow the principle and ignore the individual case. A principle, as I ought to know, is only a guideline. So I have decided, Miss Elsinger, that I will call you Mikey. From now on. I apologize for how long it has taken me to see the wrongness of my choice. The forest," Mrs. Chemsky announced, "is not going to be destroyed for the loss of one tree. It may even be improved."

"Yes, Mrs. Chemsky," Margalo agreed and, "Really?" Mikey said. "Are you really?"

"Yes," Mrs. Chemsky said. "Yes, Mikey, I am really."

"Great," Mikey said. "That's — thank you, Mrs. Chemsky." She was too surprised and pleased to even find a smile to plaster onto her face.

"Moreover," Mrs. Chemsky said, and she took her hands out of her pockets to stand up straight, like a soldier reporting in, and tell them while she looked over their heads to the back of the room, "I am going to be honest about something. I trust that you will keep this information to yourselves, and I believe that I can trust you. Steven Chemsky," she announced to the cubbies, "is my brother."

The cubbies had no reaction but Margalo did. "What about your hus —?"

Mrs. Chemsky didn't let her finish. "Now," she announced, "here is what will be done during today's detention. You, Mikey, will scrub the tops of those desks in the classroom that need cleaning. Abrasive cleanser and sponges have been left in a bucket for you, outside the janitor's door. You may use the girls' bathroom sink for water. You, Margalo, will have an old-fashioned kind of punishment. I want you to write one hundred times — and no tricks about this, please. Each sentence must be written out completely, one sentence at a time, and numbered, too, please. On the board, Margalo, not at your desk. Mikey will be working on the desktops. The sentence you will write is this one: *I will not start rumors.*"

"But —" Margalo started to say. Mrs. Chemsky raised a hand, palm front, like a policewoman stopping traffic.

"Did I explain myself? Did I share my thought processes? Did I justify the punishment? Did I ask you to defend or explain yourself? No, I didn't think I had." Mrs. Chemsky walked over to the hall door and opened it. "Mikey? Let's go. Get to work, Margalo."

While they did their punishments, Mrs. Chemsky corrected papers at her desk. They didn't need to be told that there was a No Talking rule in effect. There were only quiet sounds in the room. Mrs. Chemsky's red pencil moved scratchily, checking off answers on math papers, a check for correct, an X for wrong, and totaling the number of right answers. The papers rustled when she had finished one and moved on to the next. Margalo's words clacked onto the board with occasional squeaks. It felt like every time she finished a sentence, put the period in, numbered the next one — seven. Only seven so far? It would take *days* to write one hundred sentences — she was making a promise.

Probably, if she couldn't get away with it, and it looked like she couldn't any longer, this was a promise she'd better keep.

Mikey made the most consistent noise, a rubbing scrubbing sound of sponge scouring at laminated wood with abrasive cleanser. She scrubbed, and then she sponged with a sound like windshield wipers in the snow. It was sort of fun to see what various people had written onto their desktops — and she wondered if Mrs. Chemsky knew the kind of thing that David Thomas was writing. Frankly, she doubted it, because if the teacher had known, she would have erased it herself and not let a girl student see it.

But Mikey didn't much like having the work of cleaning up other people's messes.

The clock moved slowly, five minutes of the detention hour used up by the first conversation. Ten minutes gone. Fifteen. Sixteen. Seventeen.

At twenty-eight minutes, Mikey threw the sponge down into the bucket — which needed rinsing out and filling with clean warm water for the second time already. People were such pigs! She had to bend over each desk, because if she sat in the desks she couldn't get enough pressure on the sponge, to get the darkest marks out. Her back was tired.

"It's not fair," Mikey said, as she got to the doorway. "How come she doesn't have to scrub, too. And get her hands all in detergent. And carry water, and fetch it."

"How come she gets to come and go," Margalo complained. "And doesn't have to do the same stupid thing over and over, standing in the same position?" Margalo's right shoulder was getting stiff from reaching up to write the same stupid thing, over and over. "It's hard writing on the board, Mrs. Chemsky. Why can't I do this on a sheet of paper?" she complained.

"Our punishments are supposed to be the same," Mikey complained.

"Yeah," Margalo said.

Mrs. Chemsky looked up at them, not impatient, not surprised. "You're two different cases, so you have two different punishments. I thought you understood that. That was the point of the example of your names, their abbreviations. I assumed you understood," she repeated, and then went back to her work.

Mikey looked at Margalo and Margalo looked at Mikey, and they both knew they were thinking exactly the same thing. They were thinking, "Different abbreviations, but they each mean something, so that's the same." Mrs. Chemsky wasn't so smart about everything.

Mikey smiled at Margalo, *I-dare-you*, and Margalo smiled the same thing right back, like a mirror. She turned to the chalkboard and wrote, "Fifty-one. I will not start rumors," but she didn't put a period. Instead, she finished the sentence, "about Ann Tarwell going to the movies with Noah Obbink." Then she erased back, put in the period and wrote, "Fifty-two. I will not start rumors," while she thought about what other rumors she wouldn't start.

Mikey looked at the desk she was working on. Somebody had been writing notes to somebody next to her — she guessed they must be girls — on this desk. She read what they'd said.

— *After Mikey, who d'you say smells worse?*

— *Lindsey. No, Karen. You?*

— *Tanisha, she really stinks.*

— *Worse than the boys?*

— *Nothing's worse than boys ha-ha.*

Mikey would never write any private thoughts down on her desk. What if somebody else read them?

Yeah, she thought. *What if somebody else read these private thoughts. And what if* — she started scrubbing carefully. When she finished, the message to whoever sat in this desk had been turned into "you stink."

This gave her an even better idea. When she came to a desk in the third row that obviously belonged to a boy, because he had illustrated it with a picture of a woman with the kind of figure only comic-book women ever got, she read what he'd written, then pulled the desk over to the windows.

At the noise, Mrs. Chemsky looked up.

Margalo started erasing the end of a sentence: *I will not start rumors about finding asbestos in the air of the first and second grade classrooms.*

Mikey said, "I need to see it more clearly. To get it clean enough," she said.

Mrs. Chemsky looked down again, and marked an answer with a big red X.

Mikey studied the drawing, and she studied the words written below it, and she studied the arrow pointing from the words to the picture of a woman lying on her side and resting her head on an elbow.

The woman wasn't wearing any clothes. But she wasn't anatomically correct, so it didn't bother Mikey. — *HOT BABE!!!* the boy had written, with three exclamation points after it. — *Great boobs,* he'd written, and drawn an arrow to them, as if anyone might not know what he meant. — *My Girl,* he had written.

Mikey scrubbed carefully and then left the desk there by the windows, to dry if anyone were to ask her. She pulled a second desk out of the third row, and dragged Louis Caselli's desk back to replace that one, which she took over to the windows to scrub on. This left two empty spaces in the rows of desks, one of them the space where Louis Caselli sat.

She had to be quick. Time was running out. Margalo was writing number eighty-three. Mikey scrubbed the second desk clean, then took the first desk and carried it — no need to make a loud noise which would distract Mrs. Chemsky from her work — to Louis Caselli's place in the front row. She put the bucket on top of it, in case Mrs. Chemsky might look over, and see what was on Louis Caselli's desk before tomorrow morning, when Louis Caselli would be sitting there, right in front of the teacher, at a desk with an arrow pointing to the teacher's desk and a note that said *HOT BABE!!!*

Mikey could almost picture how Louis would try to keep Mrs. Chemsky from seeing what was written on his desk. She could barely wait for school tomorrow morning, watching Louis squirm, and turn red, and try to keep it covered with a book, or paper. She wished she could call Margalo over, but that was too risky.

"Ninety-eight," Margalo wrote. *I will not start rumors about Mr. Delaney being a former spy for the CIA, in Colombia.*

Mikey put all the desks back, and went back to scrubbing the last desk of the day. It was Annaliese's, and she saw there that Annaliese had put her initials, AG, in a heart with another pair of initials, CS. Which had to be Clark Smith's. There was an arrow through the heart. So she switched that desk into Clark's place, or what she thought was probably his. If it wasn't, it would be Harvey's seat or Doucelle's, and they'd make sure Clark saw the heart, with his initials and Annaliese's in it. She wondered if Annaliese and Clark would get together, on account of her interference. She wondered if she was like Cupid, when she did this. Maybe she could go as Cupid on Halloween, in a big diaper. She could get herself one of those little plastic bows at the Kmart, with plastic arrows that were tipped with suction cups. She could stick those suction cups onto people's foreheads, when everybody wore their costumes to school, or onto people's desks. Everybody would hate that.

When Mrs. Chemsky excused them at the end of the hour, Mikey made sure the teacher was on her way out of the room before she and Margalo stepped out the door to the playground. It was raining, but they'd been stuck inside all day and they didn't care if they got wet. Their mothers — Margalo's in the '72 Nova they could barely keep running long enough to run errands in, with all the little boys and girls bouncing around in the backseat, being irritating and noisy so she'd be feeling cross and depressed when Margalo got into the car, with four more detentions still to go; and Mikey's in her year-old Audi, with heated seats and a sunroof, cross because she had to leave work early — would be waiting around front, at the end of the sidewalk, where the buses parked. Mikey and Margalo went around the side of the school building, heading for their mothers. "Listen," Mikey said to Margalo, just as Margalo said, "Listen."

Each waited, until "What?" Margalo said and "What?" Mikey said.

They waited again, until "I wanted to ask you," Margalo said while Mikey started, "Can you —" and they finished together, "Spend the night?" They laughed, "This weekend?" speaking together.

"Which shall we do?" they asked, and Mikey answered, "Both. Friday night at your house, and Saturday at mine. Mine'll be the most quiet, and private. I bet."

"Mine'll be the most happening," Margalo maintained.

"So all we have to do is decide if we want excitement first or finally," Mikey said. "I want it first."

Margalo, who didn't agree, didn't argue about it. Mostly, she didn't argue because something much more interesting had occurred to her. "Did you *hear* what she told us?"

They were on the sidewalk, and both cars waited impatiently. Margalo's car waited more noisily and Mikey's more musically, but both were ready to move on along.

Mikey started to jog. "About my name? I sure did."

Margalo jogged alongside and shook her head no. "About her husband. Promise —"

Mikey stopped dead in her tracks. "The soccer game! I can't play!"

"Why?"

"Because of detention! It's all your fault!"

Margalo didn't bother saying anything.

"So what are you going to do about it?"

"What?"

"You better think of something." Then Mikey smiled, self-satisfied and confident. "You'll think of something. I'll call you. Is your phone listed?"

Both cars honked, one after the other. Two passenger doors were opened from inside.

"Are you in the phone book?" Margalo asked. "Under new listings?" she called over to Mikey, who was calling, "Directory assistance for new listings."

Both of their mothers greeted them with the same question: "Was that her?" And with the same remark: "But she looks perfectly ordinary. She looks like a nice girl."

Mikey didn't disillusion her mother, and neither did Margalo.

About the Author

I am entering Margalo and Mikey into the lists of bad girls. Girls with an attitude. Girls up to no good.
— Cynthia Voigt

Cynthia Voigt is a renowned author of books for preteens and young adults. She has written twenty-one novels, including *Dicey's Song*, winner of the Newbery Medal, *A Solitary Blue*, a Newbery Honor Book, *David and Jonathan*, *The Wings of a Falcon*, and most recently *When She Hollers*, a Parents' Choice Award-winner. She is also the recipient of the 1995 *SLJ/YALSA* Margaret A. Edwards Award for Outstanding Literature for Young Adults.

Mrs. Voigt lives in Maine with her husband and the younger of her two children.